SPOOKY STORIES

An anthology of uncanny tales by
master storytellers of the weird
and unforeseen . . .

Also by Barbara Ireson
PUZZLES, GAMES AND RHYMES
and published by Carousel Books

Spooky Stories

Edited by

Barbara Ireson

Illustrated by John Hutchinson

CAROUSEL BOOKS
A DIVISION OF TRANSWORLD PUBLISHERS LTD

SPOOKY STORIES
A CAROUSEL BOOK 0 552 52055 1

First publication in Great Britain

PRINTING HISTORY
Carousel edition published 1975
Carousel edition reprinted 1976

Anthology copyright © Barbara Ireson 1975
Illustrations copyright © Transworld Publishers 1975

This book is set in Baskerville 12/13 pt.

Carousel Books are published by Transworld Publishers, Ltd.,
Century House, 61–63 Uxbridge Road, Ealing, London W5 5SA

Made and printed in Great Britain by
Richard Clay (The Chaucer Press), Ltd., Bungay, Suffolk.

ACKNOWLEDGEMENTS

Brownie by R. Chetwynd-Hayes. Originally published by Mayfair Books. Copyright © R. Chetwynd-Hayes.

Napoleon's Hat by Evelyn Fabyan from *The Third Ghost Book* edited by Cynthia Asquith. Originally published by Barrie & Jankins. Copyright © Evelyn Fabyan.

The Rain-Lady and the Ghost by Adele de Leeuw from *Legends and Folk Tales of Holland*. Originally published by Thomas Nelson Inc. Copyright © Adele de Leeuw.

The Bull by Rachel Hartfield from *The Third Ghost Book* edited by Cynthia Asquith. Originally published by Barrie Jenkins. Copyright © Rachel Hartfield.

The Water Ghost of Harrowby Hall by John Kendrick Bangs from *The Water Ghost and Others*. Originally published by Harper & Row Publishers Inc. Copyright © Harper Bros.

Curfew by Lucy Boston. Copyright © Lucy Boston.

Yi Chang and the Haunted House by Eleanore M. Jewett from *Which was Witch?*. Originally published by Viking Press Inc. Copyright © Viking Press Inc.

Spooks of the Valley by Louis C. Jones. Originally published by Houghton Mifflin Inc. Copyright © Louis C. Jones.

The Water Woman and her Lover by Ralph Prince from the BIM magazine edited by Frank Collymore. Copyright © Ralph Prince.

CONTENTS

BROWNIE

R. Chetwynd-Hayes

The house was built of grey stone, and stood on the edge of a vast moor; an awesome, desolate place, where the wind roared across a sea of heather and screamed like an army of lost souls.

Our father drove into a muddy, weed-infested drive, then braked to a halt. He smiled over his shoulder at Rodney and me, then said cheerfully: 'You'll be very happy here.'

We had grave doubts. On closer inspection the stonework was very dirty, the paintwork was flaking, and generally the house looked as unrelenting as the moor that lay beyond. Father opened the door and got out, his face set in that determinedly cheerful expression parents assume whenever they wish to pretend that all is well, even though appearances suggest otherwise.

'Fine people, Mr and Mrs Fairweather.' He gripped Rodney's arm, then mine, and guided us up a flight of stone steps towards a vast, oak door. 'You'll love 'em. Then, there are all those lovely moors for you to play on. Wish I was staying with you, instead of going back to India. But duty calls.'

He was lying, we both knew it, and perhaps the knowledge made parting all the more sad. He raised a bronzed hand, but before he could grasp the knocker, the door creaked open and there stood Mrs Fairweather.

'Major Sinclair.' She stood to one side for us to enter. 'Come in, Sir, and the young 'uns. The winds like a knife, and cuts a body to the bone.'

The hall was large, bare, lined with age-darkened oak panels; doors broke both walls on either side of a massive staircase, and there was an old, churchy smell.

'Come into the kitchen with you,' Mrs Fairweather commanded, 'that being the only room that's livable in on the ground floor. The rest is locked up.'

The kitchen lay behind the staircase; a grandfather of all kitchens, having a red tiled floor, a spluttering iron range that positively shone from frequent applications of black lead, and an array of gleaming copper saucepans hanging on brass hooks over the mantelpiece.

A tall, lean old man was seated behind a much-scrubbed deal table. He rose as we entered, revealing that he wore a dark blue boiler suit and a checked cloth cap.

'Fairweather,' his wife snapped, 'where's yer manners? Take yer cap off.'

Mr Fairweather reluctantly, or so it appeared to me, took off his cap, muttered some indistinguishable words, then sat down again. Mrs Fairweather turned to Father.

'You mustn't mind him, Sir. He's not used to company, but he's got a heart. I'll say that for him. Now, Sir, is there anything you'd like to settle with me before you leave?'

'No,' Father was clearly dying to be off, 'the extra sum we agreed upon will be paid by Simpson & Brown on the first of every month. The girl I engaged as governess will arrive tomorrow. Let me see,' he consulted a notebook, 'Miss Rose Fortesque.' He put the notebook away. 'I think that's all.'

'Right you are, Sir,' Mrs Fairweather nodded her grey head, 'I expect you'll want to say a few words to the little fellows before you leave, so me and Fairweather will make ourselves scarce. Fairweather ...' The old man raised his head.

'Come on, we'll make sure the chicken are bedded down.'

Mr Fairweather followed her out through the kitchen doorway, muttering bad-temperedly, and we were left alone with Father, who was betraying every sign of acute discomfort.

'Well, boys,' he was still determined to appear cheerful, 'I guess this is goodbye. You know I'd have loved to have taken you with me, but India is no place for growing boys, and now your mother has passed on there'd be no one to look after you. You'll be comfortable enough here, and Miss Fortesque will teach you all you need to know before you go to school next autumn. O.K.?'

I felt like choking, but Rodney, who had a far less emotional nature, was more prepared to deal with events of the moment.

'Do we own this house, father?'

'I own this house,' father corrected gently, 'and no doubt you will one day. As I told you, Mr and Mrs Fairweather are only caretakers, and they are allowed to cultivate some of the ground for their own use. Back before the days of Henry the Eighth, the house was a monastery, but since the Reformation it's been a private house. Your great uncle Charles was the last of our family to live here. I've never found the time to bring the old place up to scratch, so it has stood empty, save for the Fairweathers, since he died.'

'Pity,' said Rodney.

'Quite,' Father cleared his throat. 'Well, I expect the old ... Mrs Fairweather has a good hot meal waiting for you, so I'll push off.' He bent down and kissed us lightly on the foreheads, then walked briskly to the kitchen door. 'Mrs Fairweather, I'm off.'

The speed with which the old couple re-appeared suggested the chicken must be bedded down in the hall. Mr Fairweather made straight for his seat behind the table, while his wife creased her stern face into a polite smile.

'So you'll be going, Sir. I hope it won't be too long before we see you again.'

'No indeed.' Father shook her hand, his expression suddenly grave. 'No time at all. 'Bye, boys, do what the good Mrs Fairweather tells you. Goodbye, Fairweather.' He could not resist a bad joke. 'Hope it keeps fine for you.'

The old man half rose, grunted, then sat down again. Mrs Fairweather preceded Father into the hall. We heard the front door open, then the sound of father's car; the crunch of gravel as he drove away. He was gone. We never saw him again. He was killed on the Indian North West Frontier fighting Afghanistan tribesmen, and, had he been consulted, I am certain that is the way he would have preferred to die. He was, above all, a soldier.

As Mrs Fairweather never failed to stress, food at Sinclair Abbey was plain, but good. We ate well, worked hard, for Mr Fairweather saw no reason why two extra pairs of hands should not be put to gainful employment, and above all, we played. An old, almost empty house is an ideal playground for two boys. The unused rooms, whenever we could persuade Mrs Fairweather to unlock the doors, were a particular joy. Dust-shrouded furniture crouched like beasts of prey against walls on which the paper had long since died. In the great dining room were traces of the old refectory where medieval monks had dined before Henry's henchmen had cast them out. One stained-glass window, depicting Abraham offering up Isaac as a sacrifice, could still be seen through a veil of cobwebs; an oak, high-backed chair, surmounted by a crucifix, suggested it had once been the property of a proud abbot. For young, enquiring eyes, remains of the old monastery could still be found.

Rose Fortesque came, as Father had promised, the day after our arrival. Had we been ten years older, doubtless we would have considered her to be a slim, extremely pretty, if somewhat retiring girl. As it was, we found her a great disappointment. Her pale, oval face, enhanced by a pair of rather blue sad eyes, gave the impression she was always on the verge of being frightened, the result possibly of being painfully shy.

Where Father had found her I have not the slightest idea. More than likely at some teacher's agency, or wherever prospective governesses parade their scholastic wares, but of a certainty, she was not equipped to deal with two high-spirited boys. It took but a single morning for us to become aware of this fact, and with the cruelty of unthinking youth, we took full advantage of the situation. She was very frightened after finding a frog in her bed, and a grass snake in her handbag, and from then onwards, she watched us with sad, reproachful eyes.

It was fully seven days after our arrival at Sinclair Abbey when we first met Brownie. Our bedroom was way up under the eaves, a long, barren room, furnished only by our two beds, a wardrobe, and two chairs, Mrs Fairweather having decided mere boys required little else. There was no electricity in that part of the house. A single candle lit us to bed, and once that was extinguished, there was only the pale rectangle of a dormer window which, in the small hours, when the sky was clear, allowed the moon to bathe the room in a soft, silver glow.

I woke up suddenly, and heard the clock over the old stables strike two. It was a clear, frosty night, and a full moon stared in through the window, so that all the shadows had been chased into hiding behind the wardrobe, under the beds, and on either side of the window. Rodney was snoring, and I was just considering the possibility of throwing a boot at him, when I became aware there was a third presence in the room. I raised my head from the pillow. A man dressed in a monk's robe was sitting on the foot of my bed. The funny thing was, I couldn't feel his weight, and I should have done so, because my feet appeared to be underneath him.

I sat up, but he did not move, only continued to sit motionless, staring at the left hand wall. The cowl of his robe was flung back to reveal a round, dark-skinned face, surmounted by a fringe of black curly hair surrounding a bald patch that I seemed to remember was called a tonsure. I was frightened, but pretended I wasn't. I whispered:

'Who are you? What do you want?'

The monk neither answered nor moved, so I tried again, this time a little louder.

'What are you doing here?'

He continued to sit like a figure in a wax museum, so I decided to wake Rodney—no mean task for he slept like Rip van Winkle. My second shoe did the trick and he woke protesting loudly:

'Wassat? Young Harry, I'll do you.'

'There's a man sitting on the foot of my bed, and he won't move.'

'What!' Rodney sat up, rubbed his eyes, then stared at our silent visitor. 'Who is he?'

'I don't know. I've asked him several times, but he doesn't seem to hear.'

'Perhaps he's asleep.'

'His eyes are open.'

'Well,' Rodney took a firm grip of my shoes, 'we'll soon find out.' And he hurled the shoes straight at the brown-clad figure.

Neither of us really believed what our eyes reported: the shoe went right through the tonsured head and landed with a resounding smack on a window pane. But still there was no response from the monk, and now I was so frightened my teeth were chattering.

'I'm going to fetch Mrs Fairweather,' Rodney said after a while, 'she'll know what to do.'

'Rodney,' I swallowed, 'you're not going to leave me alone with—him, are you?'

Rodney was climbing out of the far side of the bed.

'He won't hurt you, he doesn't move, and if he does you can belt under the bed. I say, chuck the candle over, and the matches, I've got to find my way down to the next floor.'

Left alone, I studied our visitor with a little more attention than formerly, for, as he appeared to be harmless, my fear was gradually subsiding.

I knew very little about monks, but this one seemed to be a rather shabby specimen; his gown was old, and there was even a small hole in one sleeve, as if he indulged in the bad habit of leaning his elbows on the table. Furthermore, on closer inspection—and by now I had summoned up enough courage to crawl forward a short way along the bed—he was in need of a shave. There was a distinct stubble on his chin, and one hand, that rested on his knee, had dirt under the finger nails. Altogether, I decided, this was a very scruffy monk.

Rodney had succeeded in waking the Fairweathers. The old lady could be heard protesting loudly at being disturbed, and an occasional rumble proclaimed that Mr Fairweather was not exactly singing for joy. Slippered feet came padding up the stairs, and now Mrs Fairweather's unbroken tirade took on recognisable words.

'I won't have him lurking around the place. It's more than I'm prepared to stand, though why two lumps of boys couldn't have chased him out, without waking a respectable body from her well-earned sleep, I'll never know.'

'But he doesn't move,' Rodney's voice intervened.

'I'll move him.'

She came in through the doorway like a gust of wind, a bundle of fury wrapped in a flowered dressing gown, and in one hand she carried a striped bath towel.

'Get along with you.' She might have been shooing off a stray cat. 'I won't have you lurking around the house. Go on—out.'

The words had no effect, but the bath towel did. Mrs Fairweather waved it in, or rather through, the apparition's face. The figure stirred, rather like a clockwork doll making a first spasmodic move, then the head turned and a look of deep distress appeared on the up to now emotionless face. The old lady continued to scold, and flapped the towel even more vigorously.

'Go on, if I've told you once, I've told you a hundred times, you're not to bother respectable folk. Go where you belong.'

The monk flowed into an upright position; there is no other word to describe the action. Then he began to dance in slow motion towards the left hand wall, Mrs Fairweather pursuing him with her flapping towel. It was a most awesome sight; first the left leg came very slowly upwards, and seemed to find some invisible foothold, then the right drifted past it, while both arms gently clawed the air. It took the monk some three minutes to reach the left hand wall; a dreadful, slow, macabre dance, performed two feet above floor level, with an irate Mrs Fairweather urging him on with her flapping towel, reinforced by repeated instructions to go, and not come back, while her husband, ludicrous in a white flannel nightgown, watched sardonically from the doorway.

The monk at last came to the wall. His left leg went through it, then his right arm, followed by his entire body. The last we saw of him was the heel of one sandal, which had a broken strap. Mrs Fairweather folded up her bath towel and, panting from her exertions, turned to us.

'That's got shot of him, and you won't be bothered again tonight. Next time he comes, do what I did. Flap something in his face. He doesn't like that. Nasty, dreamy creature, he is.'

'But ...' Rodney was almost jumping with excitement, '... what ... who is he?'

'A nasty old ghost, what did you imagine he was?' Mrs Fairweather's face expressed profound astonish-

ment at our ignorance; 'one of them old monks that used to live here, donkey's years ago.'

'Gosh,' Rodney eyed the wall through which the monk had vanished, 'do you mean he'll come back?'

'More than likely.' The old lady had rejoined her husband in the doorway. 'But when he does, no waking me out of a deep sleep. Do as I say, flap something in his face, and above all, don't encourage him. Another thing,' she paused and waved an admonishing finger, 'there's no need to tell that Miss Fortesque about him. She looks as if she's frightened of her own shadow as it is. Now go to sleep, and no more nonsense.'

It was some time before we went to sleep.

'Harry,' Rodney repeated the question several times, 'what is a ghost?'

I made the same answer each time.

'I dunno.'

'It seems a good thing to be. I mean, being able to go through walls and dance in the air. I'd make Miss Fortesque jump out of her skin. I say, she must sleep like a log.'

'Her room is some distance away,' I pointed out.

'Still, all that racket I was making. . .' He yawned. 'Tomorrow, we'll ask her what a ghost is.'

'Mrs Fairweather said we were not to tell her about the ghost.'

'There's no need to tell her we've seen one, stupid. Just ask her what it is.'

Rodney tacked the question on to Henry the Eighth's wives next morning.

'Name Henry the Eighth's wives,' Miss Fortesque had instructed. Rodney had hastened to oblige.

'Catherine of Aragon, Anne Boleyn, Jane Seymour, Anne of Cleves, Catherine Howard, and Catherine Parr who survived him, but it was a near thing. Please,

Miss Fortesque, what is a ghost?'

'Very good,' Miss Fortesque was nodding her approval, then suddenly froze. 'What!'

'What is a ghost?'

The frightened look crept back into her eyes, and I could see she suspected some horrible joke.

'Don't be silly, let's get on with the lesson.'

'But I want to know,' Rodney insisted, 'please, what is a ghost?'

'Well,' Miss Fortesque still was not happy, but clearly she considered it her duty to answer any intelligent question, 'it is said, a ghost is a spirit who is doomed to walk the earth after death.'

'Blimey!' Rodney scratched his head, 'a ghost is dead?'

'Of course—at least, so it is said. But it is all nonsense. Ghosts do not exist.'

'What!' Rodney's smile was wonderful to behold, 'you mean—you don't believe ghosts exist?'

'I know they don't,' Miss Fortesque was determined to leave the subject before it got out of hand. 'Ghosts are the result of ignorant superstition. Now, let us get on. Harry this time. How did Henry dispose of his wives?'

I stifled a yawn.

'Catherine of Aragon divorced, Anne Boleyn beheaded, Jane Seymour died, Anne of Cleves divorced, Catherine Howard beheaded, Catherine Parr. . . .'

'I say, Harry,' Rodney remarked later that day, 'I bet Brownie was the odd man out.'

'Who?'

'Brownie, the monk. There's always one in big establishments. You remember at prep school last year, that chap Jenkins. He was lazy, stupid, never washed. The chances are, Brownie was the odd man out among the other monks. Probably never washed or shaved unless he was chivvied by the abbot, then when he died he hadn't the sense to realise there was some other place for him to go. So, he keeps hanging about here. Yes, I guess that's it. Brownie was the stupid one.'

'I don't think one should flap a towel in his face,' I said, 'it's not polite.'

'You don't have to be polite to a ghost,' Rodney scoffed, 'but I agree it's senseless. Next time he comes we'll find out more about him. I mean, he's not solid, is he? You saw how the towel went right through his head.'

It was several weeks before Brownie came again, and we were a little worried that Mrs Fairweather had frightened him away for good. Then one night I was awakened by Rodney. He was standing by my bed, and as I awoke he lit the candle, his hand fair shaking with excitement.

'Is he back?' I asked, not yet daring to look for myself. 'Yep,' Rodney nodded, 'on the foot of your bed, as before. Come on, get up, we'll have some fun.'

I was not entirely convinced this was going to be fun, but I obediently clambered out of bed, then with some reluctance turned my head.

He was there, in exactly the same position as before, seated sideways on the bed, the cowl slipped back on to his shoulders, and staring at the left hand wall.

'Why does he always sit in the same place?' I asked in a whisper.

'I expect this was the room he slept in, and more than likely his bed was in the same position as yours. I say, he does look weird. Let's have a closer look.'

Holding the candlestick well before him, Rodney went round the bed and peered into the monk's face. Rather fearfully, I followed him.

The face was podgy, deeply tanned, as though its owner had spent a lot of time out of doors, and the large brown eyes were dull and rather sad.

'I told you so,' Rodney said with a certain amount of satisfaction, 'he's stupid, spent most of his time day dreaming while the other monks were chopping wood, getting in the harvest, or whatever things they got up to. I bet they bullied him, in a monkish sort of way.'

'I feel sorry for him,' I said, 'he looks so sad.'

'You would.' Rodney put the candle down. 'Let's see what he's made of. Punch your hand into his ribs.'

I shook my head. 'Don't want to.'

'Go on, he won't hurt you. You're afraid.'

'I'm not.'

'Well, I'm going to have a go. Stand back, and let the dog see the rabbit.'

He rolled up his pyjama sleeve, took a deep breath, then gently brought his clenched fist into contact with the brown robe.

'Can't feel a thing,' he reported. 'Well, here goes.'

Fascinated, I saw his arm disappear into Brownie's stomach; first the fist, then the forearm, finally the elbow.

'Look round the back,' Rodney ordered, 'and see if my hand is sticking out of his spine.'

With a cautious look at Brownie's face, which so far had displayed no signs that he resented these liberties taken with his person, I peered round the brown-covered shoulders. Sure enough, there was Rodney's hand waving at me from the middle of the monk's back.

I nodded. 'I can see it.'

'Feels rather cold and damp,' Rodney said, and brought his arm out sideways. 'As I see it, nothing disturbs him unless something is flapped in his face. I expect the monks used to flap their robes at him, when they wanted to wake him up. Now you try.'

With some misgivings, I rolled up my sleeve and pushed my arm into Brownie's stomach, being careful to close my eyes first. There was an almost indefinable feeling of cold dampness, like putting my arm out of a window early on a spring morning. I heard Rodney laugh, and opened my eyes.

'I'm going in head first,' he announced.

Before I had time to consider what he intended to do, he had plunged his head through Brownie's left ribs, and in next to no time I saw his face grinning at me from the other side. It was really quite funny and, forgetting my former squeamishness, I begged to be allowed to have a go.

'All right,' Rodney agreed, 'but you start from the other side.'

We played happily at 'going through Brownie' for the next twenty minutes. Sideways, backwards, feet first, we went in all ways—the grand climax came when Rodney took up the same position as Brownie, and literally sat inside him. But there was one lesson we learnt; Brownie was undisturbed by our efforts, as long as his head was not touched. Once Rodney tried to reach up and sort of look through the phantom's eyes. At once the blank face took on an expression of intense alarm, the eyes moved, the mouth opened, and had not Rodney instantly withdrawn, I'm certain the ghost would have started his slow dance towards the left hand wall.

But there is a limit to the amount of amusement one can derive from crawling through a ghost. After a while we sat down and took stock of the situation.

'I wonder if he would be disturbed if we jumped in him,' Rodney enquired wistfully.

I was against any such drastic contortion. 'Yes, it would be worse than flapping a towel in his face.'

'I suppose so,' Rodney relinquished the project with reluctance, then his face brightened. 'I say, let's show him to Miss Fortesque.'

'Oh no!' My heart went out to that poor, persecuted creature.

'Why not? In a way we would be doing her a service. After all, she doesn't believe in ghosts. It does people good to be proved they're wrong.'

'I dunno.'

'I'm going to her room,' Rodney got up, his eyes alive with mischievous excitement. 'I'll say there is someone in our room—no that won't do—I'll say you've got tummy ache.'

'But that's a lie,' I objected.

'Well, you might have tummy ache, so it's only half a lie. You stay here, and don't frighten Brownie, in fact don't move.'

Thankfully, he left me the lighted candle, having thoughtfully provided himself with a torch, for there was no moon, and being alone in the dark with Brownie was still an alarming prospect. I sat down at the phantom's feet and peered up into that blank face. Yes, it was a stupid face, but can a person be blamed for being stupid? Apart from that, his eyes were very sad, or so they appeared to me, and I began to regret the silly tricks we had played on him. Minutes passed, then footsteps were ascending the stairs; Rodney's voice could be heard stressing the gravity of my mythical stomach ache, with Miss Fortesque occasionally interposing with a soft-spoken enquiry.

Rodney came in through the doorway, his face shining with excitement. Miss Fortesque followed, her expression one of deep concern. She stopped when she saw Brownie. Her face turned, if possible, a shade paler, and for a moment I thought she would faint.

'Who . . .?' she began.

'Brownie,' Rodney announced. 'He's a ghost.'

'Don't talk such nonsense. Who is this man?'

'A ghost,' Rodney's voice rose. 'He is one of the monks who lived here ages ago. Look.'

He ran forward, stationed himself before the still figure and plunged his arm into its chest. Miss Fortesque gasped: 'Oh,' just once before she sank down on to the bed and closed her eyes. The grin died on Rodney's face, to be replaced by a look of alarmed concern.

'Please,' he begged, 'don't be frightened, he won't hurt you, honestly. Harry and I think he's lost. Too stupid to find his way to. . . .' he paused, 'to wherever he ought to go.'

Miss Fortesque opened her eyes and took a deep breath. Though I was very young, I admired the way she conquered her fear, more, her abject terror, and rose unsteadily to her feet. She moved very slowly to where Brownie sat, then stared intently at the blank face.

'You have done a dreadful thing,' she said at last, 'to mock this poor creature. I am frightened, very frightened, but I must help him. Somehow. I must help him.'

'How?' enquired Rodney.

'I don't know.' She moved nearer and peered into the unblinking eyes. 'He looks like someone who is sleep-walking. How do you rouse him?'

'Touch his head. Mrs Fairweather flaps a towel in his face.'

Miss Fortesque raised one trembling hand and waved it gently before Brownie's face. He stirred uneasily, his eyes blinked, then, as the hand was waved again, flowed slowly upwards. Miss Fortesque gave a little cry and retreated a few steps.

'No.' She spoke in a voice only just above a whisper. 'Please, please listen.'

Brownie was already two feet above floor level, but he paused and looked back over one shoulder, while a look of almost comical astonishment appeared on his face.

'Please listen,' Miss Fortesque repeated, 'you can hear me, can't you?'

A leg drifted downwards, then he rotated so that he was facing the young woman, only he apparently forgot to descend to floor level. There was the faintest suggestion of a nod.

'You shouldn't be here,' Miss Fortesque continued. 'You, and . . . all your friends, died a long time ago. You ought to be . . . somewhere else.'

The expression was now one of bewilderment and Brownie looked helplessly round the room; his unspoken question was clear.

'Not in this house,' she shook her head, 'perhaps in heaven, I don't know, but certainly in the place where one goes after death. Can't you try to find it?'

The shoulders came up into an expressive shrug, and Rodney snorted.

'I told you, he's too stupid.'

'Will you be quiet,' Miss Fortesque snapped, 'how can you be so cruel?' She turned to Brownie again. 'Forgive them, they are only children. Surely the other monks taught you about. . . . Perhaps you did not understand. But you must leave this house. Go——' She gave a little cry of excitement, 'Go upwards! I'm sure that's right. Go up into the blue sky, away from this world; out among the stars, there you'll find the place. Now, I'm absolutely certain. Go out to the stars.'

Brownie was still poised in the air; his poor stupid face wore a perplexed frown as he pondered on Miss Fortesque's theory. Then, like the sun appearing from behind a cloud, a smile was born. A slow, rather jolly smile, accompanied by a nod, as though Brownie had at last remembered something important he had no business to have forgotten.

He straightened his legs, put both arms down flat with his hips, and drifted upwards, all the while smiling that jolly, idiotic grin, and nodding. His head disappeared into the ceiling, followed by his shoulders and then his hips. The last we saw were those two worn sandals. Miss Fortesque gave a loud gasp, then burst into tears. I did my best to comfort her.

'I'm sure you sent him in the right direction,' I said, 'he looked very pleased.'

'I bet he finishes up on the wrong star,' Rodney commented dourly. I turned on him.

'He won't, I just know he won't. He wasn't so dumb. Once Miss Fortesque sort of jolted his memory he was off like a shot.'

'Now, boys,' Miss Fortesque dried her eyes on her dressing gown sleeve, 'to bed. Tomorrow we must pretend this never happened. In fact,' she shuddered, 'I'd like you to promise me you'll never mention the matter again—ever. Is that understood?'

We said, 'Yes,' and Rodney added, 'I think you're quite brave, honestly.'

She blushed, kissed us both quickly on our foreheads, then departed. Just before I drifted into sleep, I heard Rodney say:

'I wouldn't mind being a ghost. Imagine being able to drift up through the ceiling, and flying out to the stars. I can't wait to be dead.'

Miss Fortesque's theory must have been right. We never saw Brownie again.

NAPOLEON'S HAT

Evelyn Fabyn

Our home, a small 18th-century château, in a remote part of Gascony, stood against a background of tall poplars, dazzlingly white in the fierce southern sunshine. A rose tree, said to be over a hundred years old, cascaded over the balustrade of the double staircase that led from the terrace to the front door. An aged wistaria climbed round the first floor windows, some of its branches having succeeded in covering part of the high reliefs on the stone pediment that decorated the façade.

I can still reconjure in my mind the rich smell of the roses, the sleepy scent of the lime trees that shaded the long straight drive, and the faint fragrance of jasmine and fern that wafted from my mother's bedroom window.

My brother once described our home as the perfect setting for a childhood, with its simple grace and peacefulness, the great vineyards where we could gorge on sun-hot grapes, and the lovely reaches of the Adour River, with the weeping willows so easy to climb up and to hide in.

I remember St Marsan in terms of gold and silver: the pale birches, the shivering shimmering poplars, the feather-like mimosas, the golden rain of the laburnum, the silvery vines, the sun-specked river.

Yet there was one place that was all darkness, fear, and mystery. A place that remained dark and creepy all through the summer's heat, a place strange, remote, secret, a long way from the house, beyond the walls of the kitchen garden, beyond the orchard and the wheat-field, halfway to the distant pine woods.

My brother and I called it, for some reason I have forgotten, Black Feets House. It was, in fact, no more than a disused toolshed, built in the days of our grand-father, who had planned to extend the gardens in that direction. It looked like a large dovecote, round in shape, entirely covered with thatch, roughly five feet in diameter.

We discovered it one day when we were playing truant from Marthe, our Basque nursery governess; I was then eight and my brother Armand was seven. Thrilled and puzzled we walked round it several times in search of a way in, to find at last, hidden by the thatch, a rusty padlock that broke away as we pulled it from the rotting wood of the door.

'You go in first,' said Armand, with what I knew to be more prudence than chivalry.

'No, you go,' I answered.

Finally, after some argument, we squeezed in to-gether and stood motionless in the semi-darkness. Huge cobwebs, almost as thick as cloth, hung above our heads; from everywhere came frightened scuffling sounds. Armand, in a shaky voice, started to sing a hymn (a thing he always did if he was frightened enough and wanted to curry favour with the Deity), while I, outwardly fearless, clutched the mother-of-pearl pen-knife in my pocket.

When our eyes had become accustomed to the dark-ness we realised that the hut was filled with treasures.

'An old tricycle,' whispered Armand, interrupting his singing, 'a big iron box, a *huge* watering-can.'

'A stone jar as tall as I am,' I answered with a shud-der as I remembered Ali Baba and the forty thieves. 'We must come back with a candle and matches.'

Relieved of the duty of having to go on exploring

we turned round and shrieked with terror as a huge bat brushed past us, like a living shudder, and then started to turn blindly in the brilliant sky.

Pale, spent but thrilled we ran home and with innocent expressions on our faces we sat on the swings, our feet dragging in the dust, whispering to one another about our secret.

'Swear,' I said, 'that even under torture you'll never tell anyone about Black Feets House.'

'Yes,' said Armand.

'Spit and say "I swear".'

We both solemnly took our oath and spat. Then we spat again several times for the fun of it.

Black Feets House was never to lose its fascination of terror, for even the candles we lit seemed to make the dark corners more eerie. We may, with time, have become accustomed to the creepy half light, to the terrifying din caused by a kick on an old water-can, to the creaks of old wood, but we never got used to the movements of invisible life, furtive wings of bats, running feet of the birds under the thatch, to our own panting breaths as we carefully moved a rotting crate that hid some horror.

Those were the days I like to remember, lovely carefree exciting days when Armand and I were children. Only one year later, soon after my ninth birthday, an event was to happen that seemed to alter the value of all things.

Armand and I were playing dominoes in the garden when our mother, in a lovely rustle of silk petticoats, came to join us before her drive. I remember the huge lace hat she was wearing, and the parasol with cherries painted on it that she twiddled round and round as she spoke. She told us that Marthe, the Basque nursery governess, would shortly be leaving and that she would be replaced by a German governess. Her name was

Fräulein Neuberg. She was coming from Hanover, where she had been employed by a Countess von Disbach, who had a daughter my age. As well as German, Fräulein Neuberg would be teaching us biology, history, the piano, drawing, and wood carving. Mother, smiling brightly, added it would all be great fun (a favourite expression of hers) then, as she turned away, she remarked on my untidy hair and Armand's dirty nails.

As soon as we had seen the carriage disappear down the drive we adjourned to Black Feets House and sat on our seats (two reversed flower-pots), allowing a lengthy silence to mark the importance of the occasion. Armand spoke first.

'I wonder what a German looks like,' he said in worried tones.

'They besieged Paris in the '70 war,' I answered, 'you know . . . when our uncle was a general.'

'Perhaps she'll be lovely with very very long fair hair she'll comb out of the window. It will hang right down on to the terrace.'

'We won't understand anything she says,' I added gloomily.

'Perhaps there'll be a train smash,' said Armand with his usual optimism.

At that moment *something very big* moved in the darkness. It moved with a deafening noise that filled the hut with appalling fear. We pushed one another, each trying to get out first, then Armand tripped over the tricycle and I fell on top of him. Something dark and furry ran past me. I heard its breath and felt its warmth against my bare legs.

Screaming, bruised, and dusty we tumbled out of the hut into the burning sunlight that hurt our eyelids after the darkness within. Armand, panting at my side, whispered as he ran:

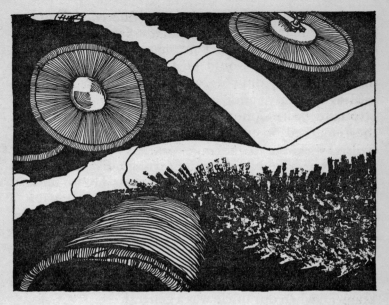

'There was something alive there. Something that overheard us. . . . I'm sure it's unlucky.'

Later, while he washed his grimy hands, I could hear him lustily singing a hymn in the cloakroom.

Until that day our world had stretched only as far as a radius of some twenty kilometres round our home. Our standard measurement of distance was the farthest farm we occasionally drove to to gather figs, nuts, or greengages. France, to Armand and me, was represented by the graceful little château, the old church and grave-yard, the Mairie with the tricolour flag fluttering in the breeze. All facts then seemed as clear as water of the Adour; everything was simple, joyous, and unchanging.

We had no foreboding of disaster as the landau, in a cloud of dust, appeared down the drive, or when Fräu-lein Neuberg alighted and bowed to our mother with something between a genuflection and a curtsey.

'This is Solange, and here is Armand,' said Mother

introducing us. Fräulein Neuberg offered me a bony hand in a black lace glove and said a few incomprehensible words in German. She then turned to Armand. He kissed her hand then tried to seize the canvas bag she was carrying, and bowed from the waist as she followed our mother up the steps and into the house.

When they had disappeared I noticed my brother's pale face.

'Isn't she *dreadful*, Solange? She has white eyes.'

'You were so polite, I thought you liked her.'

He interrupted me with an abrupt gesture.

'I was afraid,' he said.

'There's nothing to be afraid of.' I looked at the sky, blue, and flecked away with white clouds that looked like swan's-down puffs. 'There isn't going to be a storm.'

'There's going to be that woman with the white eyes,' he said grimly. 'Oh *why* didn't she die in a railway accident!'

We walked round the house in silence. By the path that led to the kitchen garden, without a word, we suddenly started to run towards the safe shelter of Black Feets House. I sat on my flower-pot, my elbows on my knees, my chin cupped in my hands.

'I haven't even *noticed* the other things about her,' I said. 'I only saw her eyes.'

'She was wearing Napoleon's hat. Fancy! Napoleon's hat! Very wide on either side, and lifted up in front. She had to go into the front door sideways, like a crab, not to get stuck.'

'I wonder what her hair's like. Perhaps she's quite *bald*.'

'How old do you think she is?'

'Quite old. About thirty.'

'She'll *never* die,' I added lugubriously. 'People live *much* older than thirty. She said something in German . . . I wonder what it was.'

Armand squared his shoulders and crossed his legs.

'I understood ... roughly, you know: it was an *incantation*. She wouldn't have white eyes if she wasn't a witch.'

'We'd better go back,' I said, 'she may want to give us a lesson at once. Isn't it all terrible!'

My voice was unsteady and I wondered if it would be belittling myself in my brother's eyes if I were to steal his thunder and sing a hymn.

Though we were not to start lessons that day, by bedtime we had been given a time-table for the week. Time for walks, play, and gathering of flowers was written in red ink. Lessons were in black, and each day at six o'clock half an hour was kept for meditation or punishments. The only bright spot of the day was that from 2 to 3.30, Fräulein Neuberg was to rest undisturbed in her bedroom. She explained that during that time she wrote letters home and worked on an embroidered cushion cover she was making for her fiancé. The gloomy time-table was hung in the schoolroom. Armand volunteered to find four drawing-pins and helped Fräulein Neuberg in putting it up. He begged for the privilege of seeing a snapshot of her fiancé and enthused in a ridiculous way as he examined a tiny black figure in front of a mass of white that were, we were told, the fiancé and the Matterhorn. He then followed her to her room to see the cushion cover. Before it was time to go into dinner I had made up my mind that Fräulein Neuberg liked Armand and that she disliked me and told him so when he joined me in the garden.

'Anyhow *why* did you have to be so *polite* to her?' (the words 'oily' and 'gushing' were not yet part of my vocabulary).

'I shall *always* be polite to her, until I've proved what she really is.'

'What she is?'

'She's engaged to the Devil.'

'The Devil!'

'Solange ... the cushion she is embroidering is all black and gold, and do you know what she told me? *She's going to fill it with hair!* Hair! *Human hair!* She'll cut all yours off, obviously, in that punishment time.'

I nervously clutched my pigtails and shuddered while Armand walked round me in a narrowing circle, his hands behind his back.

'It's no good talking to mother,' he said presently. 'She *paid* for her journey. I discovered that. She said she was pleased she was here because she would accompany her at the piano when she sang. We are alone, Solange, against the powers of the Devil. Fräulein Neuberg, for all we know, might even be a Jew whose family helped to kill Our Lord, *and* she may be the daughter of the man who besieged our uncle in Paris. She'll probably kill the dogs and the parrot and she'll certainly cut off your hair.'

'I am going to make her life so nasty that she'll pack that great trunk of hers, pick up her canvas bag, and go back to Germany,' I said.

Armand stopped his perambulations.

'You can't, you mustn't!'

'I shall.'

He clasped my arm. 'Solange, you mustn't. Please don't. Please don't.' He was about to cry, 'Promise me you won't.'

'Why shouldn't I?'

'Because if you do you'll put suspicion on to us if she dies. We'll start a secret league. We'll be the knights of Black Feets House. You can be leader as you're the elder. We'll wear an insignia under our sailor shirts and use a password when we go to the hut. We'll have a shield and our motto will be "Suck up". Every morning we'll say three times "Down with the Devil".'

He stood before me, tightening his puny fists and stamping his foot on the lawn.

Fräulein Neuberg appeared on the terrace. She was wearing Napoleon's hat, the only one she possessed and that she only took off when she dined with Mother.

'You must now your hands wash,' she called.

I pretended I hadn't heard, and gazed at a lark that was singing joyfully in the summer sky. Armand immediately walked up the steps and bowed low as he went into the house.

'Solange, do you hear me not?'

I looked round, feeling an unworthy member of the secret league I had just joined.

'Go at once and mind your hair too.'

'I know ... think of the cushion ...' I said defiantly as I went by.

It was within the next few months that we realised that the world (that lovely pattern of blue, paler blue and brown in our atlas) was divided by frontiers and that that word meant much more than a dotted irregular black line. We were to discover that Fräulein Neuberg, who appeared to be omniscient about multiplying fractions, rules of perspective, and elementary biology, affirmed that the German army was the greatest in the world, as were German musicians, German poets, and the German people.

'Ask her about the Devil,' Armand would whisper to me. 'Ask her whether her ancestors killed Our Lord.'

But I asked no questions. I just listened in a sulky silence when she quoted Heine or played Mendelssohn. Every time my hair was untidy, every time I refused to answer she told me of the perfect little girl she had taught before she came to us. Sweet little Mitzel was always good, always polite and obedient. How Armand and I were to hate little Mitzel's name! We eventually dug a little grave for her behind the swings, we read the Mass to the dead and put a wreath of nettles round a rudimentary wooden cross. After that, when little Mitzel was mentioned, we would look theatrically bereaved or burst into uncontrolled laughter.

Yet through all these dramas of our life Armand kept up his courteous manner and I kept up my sulks.

'She'll go in the end,' I'd say.

'She was three years with little Mitzel,' he would answer fatalistically. Three years ... an eternity in our young lives.

Things got worse as the months went by. Fräulein Neuberg hit my hands with a ruler during the piano lessons. She pulled the knitting needles out of the scarf I had nearly finished because I wouldn't take my eyes off her face after being scolded. She made me write out a hundred times 'I shall never again rude be' while Armand went to the dancing class.

I don't remember all that happened during that year and wonder sometimes to what extent I exaggerated the way she misunderstood me. All I know is that my scars were Armand's as well. That we both learnt to dislike and to distrust. That we both saw our values being destroyed. The beautiful village church was scoffed at. 'Ah, you wait until you go to Germany ...' The Adour, our beautiful Adour with its clear waters, run straight from the eternal snows of the Pyrenees, was scarcely looked at. 'You should the Rhine see.' When the 49th Infantry regiment passed the gates and Armand and I ran down the drive at the sound of the drums and the beating of feet, she would deliberately turn her garden chair away.

'She's got round Mother,' Armand said bitterly, 'Mother doesn't know she's engaged to the Devil.'

We did all that can be done to make a governess go. We spilled stick grenadine on her suit, Armand sat on her hat, we released a bat in her bedroom. I was always punished; Armand always got away with it. We even showed her Mitzel's grave but she merely threw the cross away and flattened the earth with her boot. The more unruly I became, the more Armand acted the virtuous little boy, and as I became more frustrated an antagonism was born between us. I called him a coward, he called me a fool. We screamed and hit one another one evening in the schoolroom. Fräulein Neuberg came in and stood staring at us from the door. I can see her now, in Napoleon's hat, her white eyes cold as icicles.

'Only French children could like that behave.'

She caught me by the arm and shook me while Armand ran out of the room.

'I hate you! I hate you!' I cried hysterically while she smartly boxed my ears. When she had let go of my arm, with tears streaming down my face like rain I rushed down the stairs and into the garden. 'I'll throw myself into the Adour,' I panted through my sobs, but a farmer's boy was slowly walking along the banks on his way home. I was running across the field towards Black Feets House when I saw Armand lying on the ground behind a hedge. I crept up to see what he was doing and found that he was holding a gun (I knew that gun, it was an old trophy of our grandfather's that hung with other armoury on a panoply in the billiard room). Armand was taking aim at some invisible objective in the distance, pulling the trigger, then pushing an imaginary cartridge into the breech and shooting again.

'What are you doing?' I asked. He lay down his gun and looked up, his face smiling and gentle, his blue eyes gay and keen.

'I'm practising shooting, as I've changed my mind and am not going to be a diplomat as Papa was or an omnibus driver or a torero. When I grow up I shall be a general, like Grandpa, and I shall fight the Germans.'

The following day was to become as important a date in Armand's life and in mine as the 14th of July in the history of our country and the 23rd of August in the history of our religion. The storming of the Bastille and the massacre of St Bartholomew were relatively trifling incidents compared with the events that happened on that June afternoon.

It had been a stifling morning. The heat in the schoolroom in spite of closed shutters and drawn blinds was wearing. Armand and I were inattentive all through the history lesson and did little more than scribble on our blotting-paper when we should have been writing an essay. Fräulein Neuberg was in a tricky mood with the ruler all the time in her hand ready to hit us across the knuckles, her white eyes continually watching us. Before the end of lesson time I was given a hundred lines to write as a punishment for yawning repeatedly and Armand was told to stand in the corner for twenty minutes. Mother didn't appear for luncheon as she was suffering from a migraine so we ate in sulky silence while Fräulein Neuberg, sitting bolt upright, Napoleon's hat on her head, slowly went through a huge quantity of food, asking for second helpings and being as slow as possible; obviously, we thought, to annoy us. But Armand and I, determined to enjoy an afternoon in Black Feets House, were careful not to get any more punishments.

When luncheon was over, Fräulein Neuberg got up, having told us to play in the Mimosa Grove as 'with such heat you should out of the sun remain'.

We held the door open for her, Armand with a low bow and I with a dirty look.

'Remember that your dear mother a headache has; no sound is to be made outside her window.'

She then left the room, sidling as she went through the door to avoid knocking her hat. As she did this she turned round just enough to catch sight of Armand and me making behind her back the rudest gesture we knew. We realised we were about to be hit and stood there frightened yet defiant. She stared at us for what seemed like several minutes, then in her slow quiet voice, devoid of intonation, she told us we would receive for our rudeness *the worst punishment we had ever had*.

'I shall expect you in the schoolroom at four o'clock.'

We heard the sound of her steps on the flagstones of the hall, then the sound died as she reached the carpeted stairs.

A few minutes later, having ostensibly made our way to the shade of the mimosas, we crept round the laburnum hedge, ran across the kitchen garden, out by the farther gate and across the field under the burning sun. We ran, sweating, panting, stumbling, suddenly seized by panic. I saw Armand's pale terrified face as we rushed forward expecting every second to hear Fräulein Neuberg's voice telling us to stop. I believe we then knew all the terrors of escaping as well as any convict flying from his gaol, as well as any prisoner of war escaping from his camp. And the fear was the greater for not having been expressed.

We stumbled into Black Feets House, pushed the door to and piled old crates and water-cans against it. Then we sat trembling on the cool ground. Armand spoke first.

'The worst punishment we've ever had,' he said. Then, horribly loudly, he began to sob, beating his hands on the floor, hiccuping indistinguishable words. I crawled towards him and tried to pacify him but it only made him cry louder. I patted his back as though he were a big dog. I scratched the back of his hair as I scratched the parrot's feathers, but I could speak no word because I was crying too. Finally his sob diminished, he choked and sniffed.

'I can't bear it!' he whispered. 'Solange, I want to die! You see *I know* what she'll do to us.'

'What?' I asked, terror rising again in my heart.

'She'll first cut your hair and then she'll *crucify* us. She'll watch us die slowly. She'll watch us with those white eyes! She hates us. We'll be dead by tea-time!'

It was a terrible picture I conjured then in my mind of Armand and I crucified and dead and Fräulein Neuberg sitting at the schoolroom table drinking Spanish chocolate and eating Genoise cake, the cherry in the middle, the bits of angelica . . . while our mother slept in her bedroom, oblivious of the horrors that were going on, a handkerchief soaked in eau de cologne on her forehead.

'What's that? Listen!' cried Armand suddenly.

I stifled my sobs and listened. We heard the low growl of distant thunder.

'A storm . . .' I whispered.

The whole hut seemed to sigh and creak with fear.

'It's a long way off,' whispered Armand.

Then there was another much louder roar followed by silence.

'We must go home,' I said. 'Mother doesn't allow us to be out in a storm.'

'We are not out,' said Armand, crouching by my side.

The darkness of the hut was suddenly lit by a terrific flash of lightning, thunder cracking the air simultaneously. We had scarcely had time to cover our ears with our hands when lightning and thunder struck again. Then the rain began to beat against the thatch like a demented thing, its sound punctuated by the awe-striking voice of the storm.

We pushed the crates out of the way and gingerly opened the door. A rush of water was turning the path into a pond. Lightning blinded us for a second as we jumped back. Thunder rolled overhead. The downpour must have lasted about ten minutes before it suddenly stopped. Silence surrounded us. The world, pacified, smelt of wet earth. The air became light, cool, and clean; a blazing sun laughed in the sky. Armand smiled and hugged me.

'We'll have to paddle out of here,' I said, pulling off my socks.

Presently, our shoes in our hands, we came out of Black Feets House and as we stopped on the threshold, dazzled by the sudden light, we saw her coming towards us. . . .

Armand dropped a sock in the water as he grasped my hand. We stood side by side, motionless, awaiting our doom. The storm had laid our panic.

Fräulein Neuberg was walking very slowly in her long skirt, Napoleon's hat casting no shadow on her face. Her white eyes stared at us. Armand's hand was moist with fear in mine. She came nearer and nearer but we were still too frightened to move. She got alongside us, then she walked on with the same slow step and without uttering a word.

We watched her disappear in the direction of the distant pine woods. When she was out of sight Armand and I started to run home. We were still carrying our shoes when we reached the house. Our mother was on the terrace and I was just about to explain the reason for our bare feet when she put her arms round our shoulders and led us into the 'grand salon'. There, having closed the door, she broke the news to us. Fräulein Neuberg had been struck by lightning as she stood by the front door a minute or two after the storm had begun. 'She died about half an hour ago.'

'Half an hour ago . . .' I said; 'where is she now?'

'She was carried up to her room when the doctor arrived.'

'But I saw her,' I said. 'I saw her *after* the storm, going towards the pine woods. She was wearing Napoleon's hat.'

'It couldn't have been Fräulein Neuberg, darling; the first flash killed her.'

'But it *was*. She was wearing Napoleon's hat,' I repeated.

Armand's voice rose shrilly. 'No, you are wrong, she was wearing no hat.'

We both then burst into tears and Armand, through his sobs, tried to sing a hymn.

Mother gave us orange-flower water and put us to bed herself, watching us with worried eyes. The doctor seemed to appear from nowhere and we heard him whispering on the landing. When he had gone Mother bent over my bed.

'You must have a long sleep, Solange, and tomorrow you and Armand will go and stay with your aunt in Mimizan. You'll be able to bathe and sail; it will all be great fun.'

No grown-up ever spoke to us again of Fräulein Neuberg and my brother and I only mentioned her once about a month after her death when we visited Black Feets House on our return from the seaside.

'She was wearing Napoleon's hat,' I said obstinately.

'She was wearing no hat,' contradicted Armand.

'She was.'

'She wasn't.'

That simple fact seemed to rise between us like a wall of fire. Armand shrugged his shoulders and looked round.

'Broken flower-pots, rotting wood, spiders, I hate this place,' he said.

I looked round wistfully.

'It seemed so wonderful when we were young ... a month ago.'

'That's a very long time.' We got up and stood a minute on the threshold. It was a lovely day. As we walked to the strawberry bed Armand was softly whistling a hymn.

It was forty years later that my mother and I stood in our night-clothes, fur coats over our shoulders, watching the end of the hideous blaze that had destroyed our home. Eighteenth-century consol tables, bedding, candelabras, clocks, family portraits, clothes, had been hurled higgledy-piggledy on the lawn out of reach of the licking flames. Of the house a German bomber had left nothing but smouldering ashes. My aged mother watched, unmoved by all this devastation. She had lost her son at the end of the first world war, in the second she had seen the invasion of her country, the occupation by the enemy, the swastika flying over our Mairie; the destruction of our home was just a material blow that she accepted with the quiet philosophy that sometimes comes to those that have suffered a great deal. She sat, in a graceful bergère, wrapped in her fur coat, watching the servants and the village people help to move our possessions to safety. As I went round, listing things, I came to a huge trunk, that had been hurled out of a window and lay open on its side.

'What on earth is that?' I asked my mother as I pulled out odd bits of clothing, a dilapidated blotter, books, old boots, gloves, and an old cushion.

'Those were Fräulein ... whatever her name was ... Oh, yes, Neuberg, Fräulein Neuberg's things.'

I stared aghast at the cushion. The black-and-gold

cushion for the Devil!

'Isn't it hideous?' said Mother, looking at it with distaste. 'I remember her telling me she was embroidering it for her fiancé. She filled it with her hair combings ... so Germanic ... disgusting....'

'But why is it here? Why are all her things here?'

'I thought I told you. After her death we made every possible enquiry to trace her family or her friends, I wrote to the British Consul in Hanover, I advertised for her but never could discover anything.'

'What about little Mitzel's mother, Countess von Disbach?'

'How funny you should remember all that. I'd had a written reference supposedly from Countess von Disbach, but when I wrote she answered she had never heard of Fräulein Neuberg, in fact having no children she had never employed a governess. The only address we had was that of the lodgings where she had lived for only a few weeks before she came to France.'

I stared at the great trunk with the miscellaneous junk carefully packed with tissue-paper and moth-balls.

'Was she wearing Napoleon's hat when she was killed?' My voice sounded unsteady.

'Really, Solange, how *should* I remember!'

I began to search the trunk, pulling out in turn a skirt, black lace gloves, a shawl, a heavy box filled with wood-carvers' tools and under it all, squashed, faded, shapeless yet recognisable, was Napoleon's hat.

'Armand was right,' I whispered under my breath.

But my mother had got up. She watched the last bits of furniture, the last portraits being carried away.

'Solange,' she said with sudden laughter in her voice, 'I shall have the stables and coach-house converted into a delightful home. I'll be able to see the Pyrenees from the windows now all this has gone.... It will be small and manageable.... It will all be such fun!'

THE RAIN-LADY AND THE GHOST

Adèle De Leeuw

HOLLAND

Not so long ago a haunted house stood near Dokkum. Every night, on the stroke of twelve, there was a most terrible noise in one of its bedrooms. No one would sleep in that room, and all the furniture had been removed from it except an old bed.

The people who lived in the house had tried to find out what caused this unearthly noise but, since no one was brave enough to stay in the room at night, it remained a mystery.

One evening, when it had been raining for a week, a little old woman came to the door. The trees were dripping, the streets were flooded, water ran in a swift stream down the road. The leaden skies seemed to have endless rain left in them. The fields had begun to look like lakes, and it was difficult to get about.

The poor woman was soaked to the skin. Rain dripped from her hair onto her shoulders. Her shoes squished with water. She had tried to put her skirt over her head as a kind of umbrella, but that was soaked, too.

She was timid about knocking on the door, but she thought, 'The people who live here can only tell me to go away—that's the worst they can do.'

But to her amazement the maid who answered the door asked the old woman to step inside. A couple of children peered cautiously at her from the other end of the hall. She beckoned to them to come nearer, for

47

she loved children, but they turned and ran away.

An old gentleman came out of the dining room. 'Would you like to spend the night here, little lady?' he asked.

'Oh, yes, please, mijnheer.'

'And you're not afraid?'

'Why should I be afraid?'

'Would you dare to sleep in a haunted room? It's the only one that isn't occupied.'

'In any room, mijnheer, even if there were a dozen ghosts.'

He looked at her sharply. 'Well, come along with me.'

As she walked beside him, the little old woman looked back and saw the trail of water she was leaving. 'It's a pity to drip over your nice floor,' she apologised.

'Think nothing of it,' he said. 'If you are willing to spend the night in the haunted room, I'll be most grateful. Then, perhaps, we'll come to the end of this mystery.'

There was nothing special about the room, except that it was furnished only with an old bed. The walls were thick, and the sill under the one window was wide. The old gentleman sat down on it, and looked at his guest thoughtfully.

'Are you sure you're not afraid?'

'If mijnheer had been walking in the rain as long as I have been, he wouldn't be afraid, either. I am far too tired to be afraid.' She watched the water dripping from her clothing on to the floor.

He said, 'I suppose you'd like to go right to bed?'

'If mijnheer would send me a towel so that I can dry myself, I will be grateful. Then I shall go to sleep in that beautiful bed.'

'*One* towel!' cried the old gentleman. 'I'll have them bring you ten!'

When she had dried herself, the old woman climbed into the bed, and fell asleep at once, despite the sound of the rain pounding on the roof. She slept right around the clock. And when she woke in the early morning, the door was opening slowly, and a little girl was peering round it.

'Come in, little one!'

'Are you the rain-lady?'

'Why, what a nice name you've thought up for me! And what's your name, my dear?'

'Annetje.'

'And how old are you?'

'Four, and next week I have a birthday.' The little girl looked at the rain-lady. 'Why aren't you dripping any more?'

'I slept between dry sheets, and I don't want even to think about rain!'

They heard a loud voice in the hall. Annetje looked frightened. 'Oh, that's Grandfather. He said that I must never come into this room.'

The old woman had forgotten all about the ghost; she decided that she had better go at once. She dressed hastily and slipped quietly down the stairs. As she was opening the outer door, she remembered that she had not thanked her host for his kindness.

When she found him, he shook his head. 'Do you mean you would have gone away without telling me what happened in that room during the night?'

'Happened?' she said. 'Nothing happened. I slept.'

'Didn't the ghost appear? Why, in *my* room, I heard that horrible racket at midnight!'

The woman said, 'Would you like me to stay in the haunted room another night? This time I'll try to keep awake to see if the ghost comes.'

'That would be fine.' He called one of the maids. 'See that our guest has everything she wants.'

That night the old woman went to bed early so that she could get her sleep before midnight. Suddenly she awoke, and sat up in bed. It was pitch-dark outside, but in the room there was a dim blue light. Where did it come from? Should she call her host?

Near the window a figure was walking back and forth. She could hear the footsteps as those of a sentry. But she felt no fear. Peering out between the bed curtains, she called, 'Who are you?'

The ghost came towards her, and held his hand in front of her face. 'Go back to sleep!' he ordered.

The old woman sighed and settled her nightcap on her head. 'Well, if you say so, I'll go back to sleep. But hurry up with whatever you're doing, will you?'

'Hmmm,' the ghost said. 'You don't seem to be afraid of me.'

She lay down again, and pretended to sleep. But she

kept her eyes half-open, and whenever the ghost looked towards her, she almost closed them. She could see him well enough between her narrowed lids. He was tall and thin, and wore a dirty cap on his sparse hair and dilapidated slippers on his feet. His trousers were ragged and there were big slits in his coat; there was a sprinkling of dust on his shoulders.

All at once, with frightening speed, he leaped on to the wide window sill. He dug his fingernails into the wood and lay there, howling. The rain-lady sat up again, but a little more cautiously than the first time.

With one bound, the ghost sprang towards the bed, and she barely had time to throw herself down again, pretending to snore, before she felt his eyes boring into her. He shook his fist at her, and his fingers rattled like dry bones.

Now the old woman was really frightened. She could almost feel his hands around her throat, and she heard his voice in her ear, saying, 'Lie still, and see nothing!'

As soon as he turned back to the window, she raised herself on one elbow and parted the bed curtains. She saw the ghost take some carpenter's tools from his pocket—a hammer, a file, a small saw. He began to work on the window sill, ripping out the woodwork below it.

Just as he tore the last board loose, a torrent of golden ducats poured on to the floor in a clinking stream. The ghost squatted and pulled more coins, of gold and silver, from a hollow place in the wall. Then he began to put the coins in piles, counting, counting, in a hoarse voice.

The little old woman hardly dared breathe, but she soon saw that his mind was only on the money. Suddenly the clock in the hall began to strike. The ghost leaped up, flung the coins back, helter-skelter, into the hole beneath the window sill, replaced the boards, and on the last stroke of midnight, he disappeared into thin air.

The woman wondered if she had dreamed what she had seen. She lay wide-awake, listening to the rain which was still falling from the dark skies, and waited for morning. As soon as it was light, she dressed and crept downstairs. A sleepy maidservant met her in the hall.

'Was the ghost there?' the girl asked.

'Yes. Tell your master to get up. There is a fortune in that room.'

Soon all the family had gathered around her. 'Tell us what happened,' they cried. But when she told them, they could not believe it.

'Go and look,' she urged. 'You will find riches there you never dreamed of.'

Even so, they would not take her word for it until they had pried up the window sill. Then a great gasp went up, for the money fell out in a seemingly endless stream. It covered the floor.

When the stream of coins finally stopped, the old woman said, 'But where did all these coins come from? How did they get here?'

The grandfather was the only one who could answer her. He said, 'In this house, long ago, there lived a miser. His neighbours did not know much about him, but they did know that he was a mean and selfish man. He drove the poor from his door rather than give them a crust. One time he even sold the home of one of his debtors just because he wanted more money.

'When he died there was no one to mourn him. Not a penny was found in the house, so he was buried in a pauper's grave. People wondered what had happened to all the money he must have had. In the great carved chests they found only cast-off clothing.

'No one ever thought of this hiding place. Who

would have imagined that money would be hidden under a window sill? That was probably why the miser's ghost came back to this room every night. His punishment must have been to count the coins over and over again, as he had done in his lifetime, until, by some chance, they were found by living people.

'Now,' the old gentleman concluded, 'I am sure he will never come back.'

'Do you really thing so?' the little old woman said. 'Then I am glad that I was able to lay the ghost.'

'Yes,' he said, 'and for that reason, and to show our gratitude, I invite you to stay with us always.'

She shook her head. 'What could I do here? No, I must go as I came.' She pulled her skirt over her head again and, without another word, went out into the rain.

The rain poured off the roof and the wind drove it in gusts down the road. The children ran to the door, calling after the woman, 'Come back, rain-lady! Come back!' But she did not seem to hear them, and disappeared into the mists.

THE BULL

Rachel Hartfield

The bull-ring, the heavy iron ring set fast in the great blocks of stone, was for me the centre of enchantment. All else rayed out from that: even the farmyard, transformed into a walled garden, was only a setting for this fabulous thing. My memories have the selective quality of childhood and I see, always in brilliant sunshine, two sides of the farmyard. There is a high white cliff, the house, and right-angled from it the second, the important side. Here I see two deserted cowsheds, and in between them a space, a red-brick terrace, where a third shed has been pulled down. Soft-coloured tiles, folded one on the other, roof the sheds; on the terrace floor the bricks are slender and old, pushed down with the weight of standing cattle. An enormous wall is at the back of the terrace. It is built with blocks of local sandstone and against it a fig tree rubs its large green hands softly over the brick. Somewhere under the branches is the ring.

Only the accident of whooping-cough could have persuaded my parents to rent the farm-house for the summer. They were orderly and disliked change and we usually went to the sea for a month. It must, therefore, have been a severe illness which exiled them for three months from town. I think, too, that they were offered the house at a low rent, for my father was a barrister with, as yet, a slender practice. He came down when he could during the summer, bumping in an iron-tyred trap from the station over the stony drive. The house was about fifty miles from London, but this is all the fact I know, for my parents are both dead, and in middle age I cannot remember the village nor the county, whether Kent or Sussex. It has always seemed to me a place out of time, existing for that summer and no more.

It is set high on a hill, the farm-house, and the oast on the south side has been built into the dwelling. The front windows are cushioned in by rolling fields, so that as I lean out, on that first evening, I can almost touch the heads of corn and walk on a yellow sea. Distant over the valley on the opposite hill, another oast points upwards, like a church steeple. There are no other houses and we are alone, with a wood of sweet-chestnut and beech and hollies crowding up behind the house and on each side of the drive. In that wood the foxes live undisturbed.

Small wonder, then, that on the first night we slept there I was restless, a London child a little frightened and strange under the thick layers of silence. My room faced south on to the farmyard, as indeed did my parents' room next along the passage, so my fear was mixed with a comfortable sense of security. I wakened once or twice early in the night and heard the thin voice of an owl. Much later I wakened again. This time I sat up because I thought I heard, vaguely, distantly, the clatter and slip of hard feet on brick, as if it were the restless movement of some animal. I heard it with a pleasurable thrill, half afraid, half excited, but it seemed not so extraordinary since I was at a farm-house. In the morning when I looked out on the deserted sheds and brick terrace, at the sun shining on a neglected garden, on tangled roses and a mulberry tree, it seemed less possible, but not particularly disturbing. I did, however, say something to my parents about it during the day. They were having coffee on the brick terrace and I was

standing by, fingering the ring.

'Did you hear an animal in the night?' I asked, 'moving about out here?'

Could my parents have exchanged a look? Certainly my mother would have looked at my father—she was completely under his spell always—before replying lightly:

'You must have been dreaming.'

It was, I am sure, on that occasion that my father got up from his chair and came over to me by the wall. Did he want to distract my attention, or was he indulging his lifelong passion for giving information? I do not know now, but I dropped the ring and ran to him when he asked:

'Have you seen this wall, these stone blocks? Look, they're completely honeycombed. It's all sandstone, and if you watch you will see the little striped wasps go in and out. No, they don't sting.'

Sure enough the old wall, here and there from end to end, was lacy and light with the tiny excavations. As I watched, a bright miniature wasp came out of a hole and sent down a slide of sand; in each of the holes I saw a grub, still and rather sinister.

'It's been going on for years and years,' my father said. 'The blocks are nearly eaten away.' He turned to my mother. 'One day the whole wall will come down. Everything is derelict here, except the house; it's beyond saving now. A pity it ever stopped being a farm.'

A pity it ever stopped being a farm, except for us and our happiness. We loved it, my mother and I, the freedom, the bright upland air, the complete relaxation when my father was in London. Convalescent now, I coughed and whooped over the large neglected gardens; we went sometimes by trap to the sea, sometimes for picnics beyond our fields to a country of bracken and forest-edge. I became less peaked and more hungry, I slept so peacefully, as a child does sleep, that I was not troubled by any fears at night. Sometimes I thought I heard, under a veil of sleep, a restlessness from the walled garden, perhaps a muted sound, like a beast lowing gently in a misty dawn. But I heard, too, from the wood the urgent bark of a dog-fox, the wood-peckers calling with the first light: all these tatters of sound merged and vanished in my quiet waking. It was in the picture now, part of the country life, of the house which had grown out of a farm.

I do not know how long it was before I made friends with the old man. I saw him leaning on our wicket gate which gave on to a field path, one day when I was playing near the sprawling rosemary bushes. He had the merry, inquisitive, nutcracker look of the very old, as though he hardly had time left to satisfy his amusement and curiosity about life. He watched me for some minutes, without any embarrassment on either side, before he asked:

'Do you like being here? I reckon you do after London.'

I said, 'Yes, of course,' and after another pause I asked him where he lived.

'Over there,' he said, indicating with his head the distant oast house. 'There's where I've lived all my life. You can't see them, but there's cottages round the farm there. I used to work here when it was a proper farm.' And he began to chuckle and I laughed too in sympathy until a fit of coughing and whooping ended it.

Then he put his head on one side and said quietly, almost to himself: 'And how's the old bull?'

I can see myself now, kneeling on a rug on the grass, my toys spread out around me. I remember I did not look up or pause in my game, but answered equally quietly, and very casually:

'He's noisy at night.'

59

The old man gave me a look, as though recognising me for the first time, and said:

'I reckon he is. He was always restless, that bull.'

Then I asked the question that had been constantly in my mind, buried under the bright, sliding days, but urgent each time I looked at the terrace.

'Did he live here? Was he chained to that ring in the farmyard?'

'Most of the year. He didn't get out much. Yes, he stayed in that shed, most of the year. It had a roof and sides then, and he couldn't see much. I used to muck it out when I was a lad, into the midden. So you've heard him?'

'Where is he, then?'

'Where is he? Dead. Sixty, seventy years ago. They shot him in the end.'

'*Shot* him?'

'Aye, for he killed someone. He got out one day and cornered the cowman, in the midden. Gored him badly and he died in hospital. Nobody could turn that bull away. Nor catch him. So they got a gun and shot him, three times.'

Did I ask, what was his name? Or did the old man go on, unprompted, his eyes turned back sixty, seventy years to that scene in the farmyard when he was a lad?

'They called him the Black Devil. He was a Friesian, nearly all black. A beauty, but restless, restless all the time. Never still, pulling and grumbling and clattering. I was scared of him; I was scared of the whites of his eyes and the way he looked at you sideways as you worked. But I had the pitchfork in my hand that day, mucking out, and I thought I could keep him in.'

'How did he get away?' I asked. 'Wasn't he chained up?'

He gave me his bright, sharp look, saying:

'No one could tell. No one ever knew. His chain had

60

come undone, somehow. I tried with my pitchfork to keep him in the shed, but he burst out. He burst out and then stood blinking and grumbling in the sun until he saw the cowman. He had him over, and under his horns in a flash. He hated that man and bided his chance to kill him.' Breaking off he said to me:

'So you've heard him?'

'At night time, yes.'

'That's right. He can't get away, somehow. He's still trying to get away.'

I remember that I did not repeat this conversation to my parents. I found the old man was regarded as feeble-minded, a harmless one whose sanity had gently given out with age; and I wanted to keep him as a friend. He was sane enough for me when he could tell so much about the bull, although he was never much good at talking on other subjects. His tongue would lose its sharpness; he would be vague and his sentences were lost, more often than not, in chuckling laughter. But of that distant, murderous day when the great bull got out, he was never tired of talking; it was a saga in the same words, over and over again, until I knew it by heart and could see, in crude childish colours: the scarlet blood, the dark sprawling figure under the horns. The bull-ring and the bull were in my secret life. I went then often to the ring and handled the heavy iron; I stood in the hollows of the bricks pressed down by generations of beasts, but which I felt had been worn by the Black Devil alone, moving, moving constantly day and night, grumbling to himself.

Suddenly it was late September and nearly time to go back to London. Autumn gales were gathering around our hill; the swallows were gone. One day the velvet butterflies tacked slowly in the sun over the hot terrace; the next, under a grey sky, rain drummed on the fig tree and the terrace was deserted. In the night a wind had spiralled up from the valley; the chestnuts were bending, and apples bumped down with their leaves and twigs. All day the wind rose until the trees swept against the sky like giant besoms. Our doors rattled— they were on latches—and the window-frames shook. I was excited and chased leaves over the lawn; my hair streamed out. But as darkness fell I was subdued and a little frightened by the constant roar.

In the night I awoke with the noise my window made, and I climbed out of bed to see if I could adjust the wooden wedge. There were changing patches of moonlight and across the farmyard the dark fig tree was clapping and rubbing its hands. Suddenly I saw a black shadow, blacker than the leaves, move sideways and I heard a chain clink. My heart was banging fast, but I stayed there, watching and shivering, until a cloud rushing across the sky uncovered the moon, for an instant only. But I saw him standing there, I saw him, the Black Devil, then not moving, his dark coat shining in that pantomime light, his broad moist nose ringed and taut against the chain. I swear he looked up at my window, the moonlight in his small unhappy eyes, and such an expression of hate, despair, rage, as I had never seen in all my years.

I lost sight of him as the moon slithered behind blown clouds. Then I was in bed with icy feet, my heart beating up under the pillow so noisily that sleep was impossible. Every now and then the wind crashed a crescendo against the doors and windows, like a directed assault on the house.

It must have been much later that I heard a rumble. It was gentle, like a distant train, like a very miniature landslide bumping and cascading. Above it, and as though through it, there was a confused stampeding, a muffled clatter of horned feet which circled in the shaft of the gale and diminished into it, further and further away. I was by then too scared to move, frozen into my bed. I did not hear the door open and my mother come in.

'Don't be frightened,' she called, 'it's only the wall. The old farmyard wall is down.'

She came over to my bed and put an arm round me.

'You're shaking,' she said, 'you're frightened.' And then, as though to reassure herself : 'It's only the wall.'

We were both still listening. The wind had quietened; and in the small silence there came the sound of a breath expelled, a prolonged sigh that ran into the wind and died. I put my face in my hands and thought my heart would break. It was beyond my understanding then, it has taken nearly half a century for me to understand, this presage of things to come, this echo of far-off miseries : the eternal cry of freedom.

Another day came and the air was sharp with diamonds, there were gnats dancing above overflowing water-butts, and shafts of sun struck the reddening trees. Robins were in their full autumn song. How could this brilliance be resisted? Even after such a night we were all in tearing spirits and went out early, over the damp ground and under dripping trees, to see the wall. Only half was down, the great yellow-white blocks sprawled across the terrace in a mess of sand and cement and broken twigs. The other half was slumped against the fig tree; blocks of stone lodged in the branches or tilted down through the leaves. But the bull-ring, the great iron bull-ring was on the red-brick terrace, flung wide of the wall, its staple angled crazily in the air. Beside it lay the block of stone which had held the staple, and it was split cleanly in two.

Later I left my parents and climbed through to the other side of the wall, to the old rose-walk, to see how it looked from there. Figs had fallen, squashed in the wet grass; there were wasps and flies buzzing over them. As I picked my way across the stones I heard my father talking to someone. His voice was facetious, on a razor-edge between condescension and impatience, and I knew then, for certain, that he too had heard, many times, the story of the bull.

'So the old bull got away at last,' he said.

There was the other voice, of the old farm-hand, quavering something I did not hear, and laughing as he spoke; and my father again, irritably:

'What does he say? What nonsense is he saying?'

Then my mother, conciliatory, half-kind, half-amused: 'He says he undid the chain, seventy years ago.'

THE WATER GHOST OF HARROWBY HALL

John Kendrick Bangs

The trouble with Harrowby Hall was that it was haunted, and, what was worse, the ghost did not content itself with merely appearing at the bedside of the afflicted person who saw it, but persisted in remaining there for one mortal hour before it would disappear.

It never appeared except on Christmas Eve, and then as the clock was striking twelve, in which respect alone was it lacking in that originality which in these days is a *sine qua non* of success in spectral life. The owners of Harrowby Hall had done the utmost to rid themselves of the damp and dewy lady who rose up out of the best bedroom floor at midnight, but without avail. They had tried stopping the clock, so that the ghost would not know when it was midnight; but she made her appearance just the same, with that fearful miasmatic personality of hers, and there she would stand until everything about her was thoroughly saturated.

Then the owners of Harrowby Hall calked up every crack in the floor with the very best quality of hemp, and over this were placed layers of tar and canvas; the walls were made waterproof, and the doors and windows likewise, the proprietors having conceived the notion that the unexorcised lady would find it difficult to leak into the room after these precautions had been taken; but even this did not suffice. The following Christmas Eve she appeared as promptly as before, and frightened the occupant of the room quite out of his senses by sitting down alongside of him and gazing with her cavernous blue eyes into his; and he noticed, too, that in her long, aqueously bony fingers bits of dripping seaweed were entwined, the ends hanging down, and these ends she drew across his forehead until he became like one insane. And then he swooned away, and was found unconscious in his bed the next morning by his host, simply saturated with sea-water and fright, from the combined effects of which he never recovered, dying four years later of pneumonia and nervous prostration at the age of seventy-eight.

The next year the master of Harrowby Hall decided not to have the best spare bedroom opened at all, thinking that perhaps the ghost's thirst for making herself disagreeable would be satisfied by haunting the furniture, but the plan was as unavailing as the many that had preceded it.

The ghost appeared as usual in the room—that is, it was supposed she did, for the hangings were dripping wet the next morning, and in the parlour below the haunted room a great damp spot appeared on the ceiling. Finding no one there, she immediately set out to learn the reason why, and she chose none other to haunt than the owner of Harrowby himself. She found him in his own cosy room drinking whisky—whisky undiluted—and felicitating himself upon having foiled her ghostship, when all of a sudden the curl went out of his hair, his whisky bottle filled and overflowed, and he was himself in a condition similar to that of a man who has fallen into a water-butt. When he recovered from the shock, which was a painful one, he saw before him the lady of the cavernous eyes and seaweed fingers. The sight was so unexpected and so terrifying that he fainted, but immediately came to, because of the vast amount of water in his hair, which, trickling down over his face, restored his consciousness.

Now it so happened that the master of Harrowby

was a brave man, and while he was not particularly fond of interviewing ghosts, especially such quenching ghosts as the one before him, he was not to be daunted by an apparition. He had paid the lady the compliment of fainting from the effects of his first surprise, and now that he had come to he intended to find out a few things he felt he had a right to know. He would have liked to put on a dry suit of clothes first, but the apparition declined to leave him for an instant until her hour was up, and he was forced to deny himself that pleasure. Every time he would move she would follow him, with the result that everything she came in contact with got a ducking. In an effort to warm himself up he approached the fire, an unfortunate move as it turned out, because it brought the ghost directly over the fire, which immediately was extinguished. The whisky became utterly valueless as a comforter to his chilled system, because it was by this time diluted to a proportion of ninety per cent of water. The only thing he could do to ward off the evil effects of his encounter he did, and that was to swallow ten two-grain quinine pills, which he managed to put into his mouth before the ghost had time to interfere. Having done this, he turned with some asperity to the ghost, and said:

'Far be it from me to be impolite to a woman, madam, but I'm hanged if it wouldn't please me better if you'd stop these infernal visits of yours to this house. Go sit out on the lake, if you like that sort of thing; soak the water-butt, if you wish; but do not, I implore you, come into a gentleman's house and saturate him and his possessions in this way. It is damned disagreeable.'

'Henry Hartwick Oglethorpe,' said the ghost, in a gurgling voice, 'you don't know what you are talking about.'

'Madam,' returned the unhappy householder, 'I wish

that remark were strictly truthful. I was talking about you. It would be shillings and pence—nay, pounds, in my pocket, madam, if I did not know you.'

'That is a bit of specious nonsense,' returned the ghost, throwing a quart of indignation into the face of the master of Harrowby. 'It may rank high as repartee, but as a comment upon my statement, that you do not know what you are talking about, it savours of irrelevant impertinence. You do not know that I am compelled to haunt this place year after year by inexorable fate. It is no pleasure to me to enter this house, and ruin and mildew everything I touch. I never aspired to be a shower-bath, but it is my doom. Do you know who I am?'

'No, I don't,' returned the master of Harrowby. 'I should say you were the Lady of the Lake, or Little Sallie Waters.'

'You are a witty man for your years,' said the ghost.

'Well, my humour is drier than yours ever will be,' returned the master.

'No doubt. I'm never dry. I am the Water Ghost of Harrowby Hall, and dryness is a quality entirely beyond my wildest hope. I have been the incumbent of this highly unpleasant office for two hundred years to-night.'

'How the deuce did you ever come to get elected?' asked the master.

'Through a suicide,' replied the spectre. 'I am the ghost of that fair maiden whose picture hangs over the mantelpiece in the drawing-room I should have been your great-great-great-great-great-aunt if I had lived, Henry Hartwick Oglethorpe, for I was the own sister of your great-great-great-great-great-grandfather.'

'But what induced you to get this house into such a predicament?'

'I was not to blame, sir,' returned the lady. 'It was

68

my father's fault. He it was who built Harrowby Hall, and the haunted chamber was to have been mine. My father had it furnished in pink and yellow, knowing well that blue and grey formed the only combination of colour I could tolerate. He did it merely to spite me, and, with what I deem a proper spirit, I declined to live in the room; whereupon my father said I could live there or on the lawn, he didn't care which. That night I ran from the house and jumped over the cliff into the sea.'

'That was rash,' said the master of Harrowby. 'So I've heard,' returned the ghost. 'If I had known what the consequences were to be I should not have jumped; but I really never realised what I was doing until after I was drowned. I had been drowned a week when a sea-nymph came to me and informed me that I was to be one of her followers forever afterwards, adding that it should be my doom to haunt Harrowby Hall for one hour every Christmas Eve throughout the rest of eternity. I was to haunt that room on such Christmas Eves as I found it inhabited; and if it should turn out not to be inhabited, I was and am to spend the allotted hour with the head of the house.'

'I'll sell the place.'

'That you cannot do, for it is also required of me that I shall appear as the deeds are to be delivered to any purchaser, and divulge to him the awful secret of the house.'

'Do you mean to tell me that on every Christmas Eve that I don't happen to have somebody in that guest-chamber, you are going to haunt me wherever I may be, ruining my whisky, taking all the curl out of my hair, extinguishing my fire, and soaking me through to the skin?' demanded the master.

'You have stated the case, Oglethorpe. And what is more,' said the water ghost, 'it doesn't make the slightest difference where you are, if I find that room empty, wherever you may be I shall douse you with my spectral pres——'

Here the clock struck one, and immediately the apparition faded away. It was perhaps more of a trickle than a fade, but as a disappearance it was complete.

'By St George and his Dragon!' ejaculated the master of Harrowby, wringing his hands. 'It is guineas to hot-cross buns that next Christmas there's an occupant of the spare room, or I spend the night in a bathtub.'

But the master of Harrowby would have lost his wager had there been anyone there to take him up, for when Christmas Eve came again he was in his grave, never having recovered from the cold contracted that awful night. Harrowby Hall was closed, and the heir to the estate was in London, where to him in his chambers came the same experience that his father had gone through, saving only that, being younger and stronger, he survived the shock. Everything in his rooms was ruined—his clocks were rusted in the works; a fine collection of water-colour drawings was entirely obliterated by the onslaught of the water ghost; and what was worse, the apartments below his were drenched with the water soaking through the floors, a damage for which he was compelled to pay, and which resulted in his being requested by his landlady to vacate the premises immediately.

The story of the visitation inflicted upon his family had gone abroad, and no one could be got to invite him out to any function save afternoon teas and receptions. Fathers of daughters declined to permit him to remain in their houses later than eight o'clock at night, not knowing but that some emergency might arise in the supernatural world which would require the unexpected appearance of the water ghost in this on nights other than Christmas Eve, and before the mystic hour when weary churchyards, ignoring the rules which are supposed to govern polite society, begin to yawn. Nor would maids themselves have aught to do with him, fearing the destruction by the sudden incursion of aqueous femininity of the costumes which they held most dear.

So the heir of Harrowby Hall resolved, as his ancestors for several generations before him had resolved, that something must be done. His first thought was to make one of his servants occupy the haunted room at the crucial moment; but in this he failed, because the servants themselves knew the history of that room and rebelled. None of his friends would consent to sacrifice their personal comfort to his, nor was there to be found in all England a man so poor as to be willing to occupy the doomed chamber on Christmas Eve for pay.

Then the thought came to the heir to have the fireplace in the room enlarged, so that he might evaporate the ghost at its first appearance, and he was felicitating himself upon the ingenuity of his plan, when he remembered what his father had told him—how that no fire could withstand the lady's extremely contagious dampness. And then he bethought him of steam-pipes. These, he remembered, could lie hundreds of feet deep in water, and still retain sufficient heat to drive the water away in vapour; and as a result of this thought the haunted room was heated by steam to a withering degree, and the heir for six months attended daily the Turkish baths, so that when Christmas Eve came he could himself withstand the awful temperature of the room.

The scheme was only partially successful. The water ghost appeared at the specified time, and found the heir of Harrowby prepared; but hot as the room was, it shortened her visit by no more than five minutes in the hour, during which time the nervous system of the young master was well-nigh shattered, and the room itself was cracked and warped to an extent which required the outlay of a large sum of money to remedy. And worse than this, as the last drop of the water ghost was slowly sizzling itself out on the floor, she whispered to her would-be conqueror that his scheme would avail him nothing, because there was still water in great plenty where she came from, and that next year would find her rehabilitated and as exasperatingly saturating as ever.

It was then that the natural action of the mind, in going from one extreme to the other, suggested to the ingenious heir of Harrowby the means by which the water ghost was ultimately conquered, and happiness once more came within the grasp of the house of Oglethorpe.

The heir provided himself with a warm suit of fur-underclothing. Donning this with the furry side in, he placed over it a rubber garment, tight-fitting, which he wore just as a woman wears a jersey. On top of this he placed another set of underclothing, this suit made of wool, and over this was a second rubber garment like the first. Upon his head he placed a light and comfortable diving helmet, and so clad, on the following Christmas Eve he awaited the coming of his tormentor.

It was a bitterly cold night that brought to a close this twenty-fourth day of December. The air outside was still, but the temperature was below zero. Within all was quiet, the servants of Harrowby Hall awaiting with beating hearts the outcome of the master's campaign against his supernatural visitor.

The master himself was lying on the bed in the haunted room, clad as has already been indicated, and then——

The clock clanged out the hour of twelve.

There was a sudden banging of doors, a blast of cold

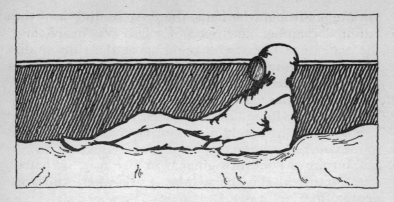

air swept through the halls, the door leading into the haunted chamber flew open, a splash was heard, and the water ghost was seen standing at the side of the heir of Harrowby, from whose outer dress there streamed rivulets of water, but whose own person deep down under the various garments he wore was as dry and as warm as he could have wished.

'Ha!' said the young master of Harrowby. 'I'm glad to see you.'

'You are the most original man I've met, if that is true,' returned the ghost. 'May I ask where did you get that hat?'

'Certainly, madam,' returned the master, courteously. 'It is a little portable observatory I had made for just such emergencies as this. But, tell me, is it true that you are doomed to follow me about for one mortal hour—to stand were I stand, to sit where I sit?'

'That is my delectable fate,' returned the lady.

'We'll go out on the lake,' said the master, starting up.

'You can't get rid of me that way,' returned the ghost. 'The water won't swallow me up; in fact, it will just add to my present bulk.'

'Nevertheless,' said the master, firmly, 'we will go out on the lake.'

'But my dear sir,' returned the ghost, with a pale reluctance, 'it is fearfully cold out there. You will be frozen hard before you've been out ten minutes.'

'Oh, no, I'll not,' replied the master. 'I am very warmly dressed. Come!' This last in a tone of command that made the ghost ripple.

And they started.

They had not gone far before the water ghost showed signs of distress.

'You walk too slowly,' she said. 'I am nearly frozen. My knees are so stiff now I can hardly move. I beseech

74

you to accelerate your step.'

'I should like to oblige a lady,' returned the master, courteously, 'but my clothes are rather heavy, and a hundred yards an hour is about my speed. Indeed, I think we would be better sit down here on this snow-drift, and talk matters over.'

'Do not! Do not do so, I beg!' cried the ghost. 'Let me move on. I feel myself growing rigid as it is. If we stop here, I shall be frozen stiff.'

'That, madam,' said the master slowly, and seating himself on an ice-cake—'that is why I have brought you here. We have been on this spot just ten minutes; we have fifty more. Take your time about it, madam, but freeze, that is all I ask of you.'

'I cannot move my right leg now,' cried the ghost, in despair, 'and my overskirt is a solid sheet of ice. Oh, good, kind Mr Oglethorpe, light a fire, and let me go free from these icy fetters.'

'Never, madam. It cannot be. I have you at last.'

'Alas!' cried the ghost, a tear trickling down her frozen cheek. 'Help me, I beg. I congeal!'

'Congeal, madam, congeal!' returned Oglethorpe, coldly. 'You have drenched me and mine for two hundred and three years, madam. Tonight, you have had your last drench.'

'Ah, but I shall thaw out again, and then you'll see. Instead of the comfortably tepid, genial ghost I have been in my past, sir, I shall be iced-water,' cried the lady, threateningly.

'No, you won't either,' returned Oglethorpe; 'for when you are frozen quite stiff, I shall send you to a cold-storage warehouse, and there shall you remain an icy work of art forever more.'

'But warehouses burn.'

'So they do, but this warehouse cannot burn. It is made of asbestos and surrounding it are fireproof walls, and within those walls the temperature is now and shall forever be 416 degrees below the zero point; low enough to make an icicle of any flame in this world—or the next,' the master added, with an ill-suppressed chuckle.

'For the last time let me beseech you. I would go on my knees to you, Oglethorpe, were they not already frozen. I beg of you do not doo——'

Here even the words froze on the water ghost's lips and the clock struck one. There was a momentary tremor throughout the ice-bound form, and the moon, coming out from behind a cloud, shone down on the rigid figure of a beautiful woman sculptured in clear, transparent ice. There stood the ghost of Harrowby Hall, conquered by the cold, a prisoner for all time.

The heir of Harrowby had won at last, and today in a large storage house in London stands the frigid form of one who will never again flood the house of Oglethorpe with woe and sea-water.

As for the heir of Harrowby, his success in coping with a ghost has made him famous, a fame that still lingers about him, although his victory took place some twenty years ago; and so far from being unpopular with the fair sex, as he was when we first knew him, he has not only been married twice, but is to lead a third bride to the altar before the year is out.

CURFEW

L. M. Boston

While my two brothers and I were at a preparatory school our parents were living abroad, so that we had to spend our holidays with relatives.

Our favourite uncle and aunt had bought a farm-house on the outlying land of an old manor, of which the estate was being broken up. The big house, Abbey Manor, was being allowed to fall down in its own good time, the owner living in a smaller dower house in the park.

The cottage which Uncle Tom and Aunt Catherine bought had also been empty for a long time. Nettles grew up to the front door and even between the flag-stones in the larder. The cottage however had been well built, with stone mullions, leaded windows, and tiled floors. It had escaped the wanton smashing up that is the fate of most empty houses, perhaps because of its isolation. A profound silence brooded over it and the acres that went with it.

My Aunt had a passion for gardening, and there was much to be done before the weed-infested land should be disciplined to her intentions, but the wildness was a paradise for children.

Walks in the adjacent park were among the excitements of our visits. There was the empty Manor with its staring windows and lost melancholy garden, its weedy paths leading to locked gates. We had Sir Roger's permission to wander there, but never climbed the gate without a thrill, or chill, of expectation. One wing of

77

the fifteenth century Manor had, with sacrilegious defiance, been built over the former Abbey graveyard. Here and there in the grounds, lying open among the rhododendrons were the empty stone coffins of forgotten Abbots, left there perhaps as being too heavy to carry away, or out of boastfulness. They were grand things, hand-hewn from solid blocks of local stone hollowed to the austerest outline of the human body

with a round resting place for the head. We passed them with great awe and even with a kind of affection, as noble things treated with contempt and now part of our private landscape.

There was also a lake, reflecting the house and the stables, which were dusty, echoing and forlorn. Uncle Tom, who liked everything ship-shape, used to sigh over all this decay, but his wife had an eye open for everything that could be moved, bought, or made use of, such as a small wrought-iron gate, a sundial, or even, in an ambitious moment, as we all stood looking up at it, the little bell tower on the stables. Its four open arches and lead dome had the beauty of extreme simplicity against the pale green sky. 'Why should it rot here?' she said. 'It would suit our yard just as well;' but the yard, surrounded by fine old barns, was Uncle's special domain and he resented intrusion. 'Rubbish,' he said, 'it's sure to be rotten. Besides I hate pretentiousness.'

On our first visit to their farmhouse Aunt Catherine had been busy making a wild garden out of an acre or two of heather and stone. It was boggy in places and we helped to make water courses for her, while she laid stepping stones and contrived rough slab bridges. There was a high mound in the middle of this patch, apparently artificial, though of some age, judging by the hawthorn tree that grew on it, and it was crowned by a large boulder. In the course of her construction Aunt Catherine needed soil to raise her beds above the level of the surrounding damp, and, resourceful woman, looking at this hillock, decided to shift the top. With what delight we responded to her invitations to see if we could roll the boulder off; but our efforts were in vain. In the end it took a team of all hands, with levers, under the personal command of Uncle in his most arbitrary mood, to dislodge it. But at last the slope took possession of it and away it rolled on a clumsy and fortuitous course and came to rest at the edge of one of our little boggy streams. 'Perfect,' said Aunt Catherine by way of thanks and dismissal.

When next we came to stay, already her heather garden was taking shape. She had perfectly preserved the wild atmosphere, and the hillock was down almost to the level of the rest. 'Look, boys,' she said, 'we struck on this yesterday.' She showed us the top of a trough or coffer stone which her digging had half uncovered. The slab over it that had served as a lid had been prized up and now rested sideways, leaving a gaping hole through which the loose earth on top had poured in.

Aunt Catherine stopped with a gasp.

'When did you open it?' she asked Uncle.

'I haven't touched it, my dear.'

'Then who has been here, and why?'

Was it a burglar? Was it treasure? We were all agog.

Aunt Catherine laughed uneasily and said she would guess that whatever was once in was now out, unless it was just old bones, and if so she was not going to disturb them.

'Old bones?' said Robert. 'It's not the right shape for a coffin. Not like the Abbots'. There's no place for a head. Perhaps it was a criminal who had been beheaded. Or perhaps it was a case of "Double him up, double him up" like Punch's victims.'

'Or perhaps an animal thing,' suggested John hesitantly. He was young and imaginative.

Robert had been rather gingerly shovelling off the clay that still clung to the lid. 'There are words on it,' he said.

We all got busy with penknives, trowel and sticks to clean the letters.

Libera nos quaesimus Domine ab Malo

Uncle Tom translated it for us. 'Deliver us O Lord from the Evil One.'

'I don't like it,' said Aunt Catherine. Then she shrugged and became practical again. 'I'm short of a slab for my stepping stones,' she said. 'This will do very well. Come on, boys. All together, lift.'

The slab took its useful place face downward in one of the paths, and the coffin itself was skilfully planted with bushes of rosemary and Spanish gorse and trailing rock-roses. By the time this story really begins it had a natural and undisturbed appearance, and around the wild garden that it dominated the lapwings and wagtails made themselves at home.

It was the beginning of the long summer holidays. Aunt Catherine having completed one plan, was now looking for something new, and the suggestion of moving the bell tower from the Manor stables was raised again. We set off with Uncle Tom one afternoon to examine it. The Manor stables surrounded three sides of a courtyard and were in atrocious condition. The once beautiful and elaborate coach house let in the rain through a hole in the roof. The loose boxes were crumbling with dry rot. Our footsteps and voices rang intrusively as we did a tour of inspection before mounting the ladder to the lofts, and we explored such of these as had floors that would bear us. Spiders and rats were all that moved there now. Uncle Tom was the first to go up the second ladder and thrust his body as far as his knees into the little cupola, while Robert and John were jostling on the lower rungs, their heads level with the opening. I was alone on a little square landing; on one side of me was the ladder, on three were doors opening into dark lofts. We had already explored them and knew them to be empty, and therefore I was very scared to hear a hoarse burst of laughter rather like a horse's cough that seemed to come from one of them. I tugged at my brothers, and they came down, including Uncle who had finished measuring and tapping. I told them there was something there, and we all went round again, and I am afraid I took care neither to be first nor last, in or out, of any of the rooms. But we saw nothing and I was mercilessly teased for my fear as we returned home.

At supper that night my Aunt heard all about it. The measurements were very suitable, the condition not bad—'Though the bell's missing,' said Uncle Tom;

'You get a splendid view of our place from the roof, Catherine; I could see your Bad Man's coffin quite plainly. There's the chap that heard him too,' he added, pointing his fork at me. 'Made us all feel quite queer. I'll go and see Sir Roger tomorrow. They say he'd sell the hat off his head if he could. I like the idea of having a bit of the old house here. Anything new looks new.'

'Don't you bring anything too old over from the Manor,' said Aunt Catherine; 'leave the ghosts behind anyway.'

'It's too late to warn me about that,' he retorted. 'It was you who took the lid off the Bad Man's coffin.'

'It was open already.'

'Well, who rolled the boulder away that was supposed to keep him down?' and again he pointed at us with his fork, and we grinned, though shudders ran down our spines.

The next day Sir Roger himself happened to pass our gate. He stopped to speak to us all, even Robert, John, and me, grimy and barefoot as we were.

'You are digging yourselves in very nicely here, I must say,' he said to Uncle. 'It all looks very jolly. I like the way you do it, too. Of course I have no choice but to sell what I can, but these gimcrack buildings do gall me.'

This was a good opening, and before long bargaining for the bell tower had begun. It ended in Uncle's favour, because at the last moment he brought out his trump card—there was no bell.

'But there being no bell is one of its greatest attractions,' said Sir Roger. 'There's a legend, you know. It was called the Judas bell, but where it originally came from and who betrayed what I don't know. It was the old curfew, and of course if people are out when they ought to be in, things are likely to happen to them.

The old people round here say the bell had a 'familiar'. The last person who rang it was my great-grandfather, who did it for a wager. And it is a fact that he was found dead. Rather horribly dead. After that the bell was taken down and destroyed.'

'Well, you can't expect me to buy a legend about a bell that is missing,' said Uncle Tom, and the bargain was settled at a very small figure.

Before the end of the holidays the graceful little bell tower was set up on the middle building in our stable-yard. Both Uncle and Aunt were pleased. It was re-painted to match its new position and looked well there.

Wet weather had set in. We had grown tired of all the games that can be played in the house. Then Robert said he would go and fish in the Manor brook and we followed with jam jars of worms. We had to cross the wild garden, which had, since Uncle's jokes, begun to stir sinister feelings in us. The lapwings cried and veered and flung themselves along the wind, the thin rain pattered in the little brown streams, and the wagtails looked sharply at us, and ran hither and thither as though disguising their real activities. We began to run, and shooed them away as if they were unwanted thoughts, but as we paused half-way across the stile into the park and looked back, there they all were as before, and the curlews sounded derisive as if we had no busi-ness there. The little stream through the park had in-vaded the grass at its edge beyond the cast of Thomas's fishing rod, and the lake into which it flowed had swol-len into damaging proportions. The cinder road that led to the Manor farm was under water, and the farmer was there with Sir Roger, bitterly complaining that it was all because the outlet sluice was blocked and had never been mended, and that the lake itself was silting up and so full of weeds you couldn't tell where it began and where it ended. Sir Roger was listening with a pained expression. He promised to have it seen to as soon as the flood subsided enough to allow work to begin. As for us, we spent the afternoon happily testing the depth of every overflow and returned home wet to the skin.

A week later dredging operations began on the lake. The sluice was opened and the water sank to mud level. The weeds were cut down, and a band of old men in waders were wheeling the smelly fibrous mud in barrows along planks. We were there of course to watch. Much came to light that would never have been expected. A sunken boat, a scythe blade, a weather vane, a skull, and most surprising of all, a bell. It was of unusual shape, but covered thickly with sharp flakes of rust. The pivot of its tongue was rusted up solid so that it could not swing.

'It's the old Judas bell like enough,' said one old man. 'Didn't I hear tell that your Uncle had bought the bell tower? That's an odd thing for anyone to buy. I'd like to hear what my old woman would say if I came back one day and said I'd bought her a bell tower.'

We ran back to announce the find at home, and Uncle Tom called for Sir Roger and took him along to look at it. Uncle had a flair for antiques, and he thought that the bell might prove to be incised in some pattern which might be curious or of interest. But Sir Roger was interested in nothing but 'Sherry and whippets', as we knew from Uncle's indiscreet conversation. 'Look at the rust on it,' he said, 'I can't take any money for a thing like that. Certainly, do what you like with it. I'm not superstitious, but I wouldn't touch it.'

Uncle shook his head at me and said we must expect the worst.

The bell was sent to be cleaned and repaired, but even in its absence we now had a prickly feeling of foreboding. I remember the golden September weather, the scent of southern wood and lavender, and the yellow leaves spotted with black that were beginning to fall. But for us the garden had become haunted. We no longer basked in it quite at our ease, or felt as heretofore that earth and fields, trees and sky were all our own. There were darker corners where we definitely did not go, where in a game of 'I spy,' for instance, nobody thought of hiding or looking.

It was on the last morning of the holidays that the bell came back. It was delivered by van, wrapped in sacking, with its now mobile tongue thickly wedged and muffled in felt. We all hung around while Uncle unwrapped it. Seeing us so deeply interested, he made quite a ritual of it, marching off to the barn with us in procession behind him. The clapper he had kept muffled till the last. It was to be 'unveiled'. When at last he pulled the first toll the sound that it gave out was so unexpected as to be quite shocking. It was a high wide-carrying note, and though it had a certain churchiness, there was in it something wild and almost screamlike. The afternote that vibrated long after within the bell sent a creeping chill up my spine. When the last sinister tingle had faded out of the shaken air, Aunt Catherine said, 'I'm certainly no going to have *that* rung for dinner. It would take away my appetite.' Uncle seemed not disposed to dispute it. He said, 'If they rang that at curfew, they gave you fair warning.'

We were to go back to school the next day, and this was a thought that blotted out all others. It was important to get the most out of the last afternoon. Towards sunset when we were playing 'I spy', I was crouching in a deep clump of red dogwood, not far from the house, holding my panting breath and listening for the approach of Robert and John. I heard their voices drawing off in the wrong direction, and was beginning to feel I had time to straighten my stiff knees before they could possibly return, and then to hope they wouldn't be too long, when with no other warning a feeling of utter isolation and panic took me. I felt I was deserted, exposed to unknown dangers, perhaps trapped. I turned involuntarily to look behind me, and saw two long-nailed soily hands begin to part the leaves, and an evil face looked in. His hair and cheeks were clotted with earth, through which his yellow teeth showed more on one side than the other, his eye sockets were appallingly hollow, and he lifted his chin as the blind do when they seek.

I shot out of the bushes like a rabbit when the ferret looks in, and ran as hard as my legs would carry me to the house. My clamour soon brought Robert and John and Aunt Catherine, to which I could give no better explanation than that I had seen a horrible face. She calmed me as best she could, saying it was probably a tramp coming in to pick up apples, and Uncle Tom should go round and send him off. Confidently she and Uncle exchanged that word as if it met the case perfectly—some tramps, a tramp, the tramp—as if a casual word like that could cover such lurking horror. Uncle Tom went striding off looking very fierce, but he came back having seen nobody.

Dusk had come. It was cold and the wind was rising, and we, as may be imagined, had no heart to play outside. So after tea Aunt Catherine let us light the fire, and we persuaded her and Uncle to stay with us and tell us ghost tales—the others I think out of pure love of sensation, and I because it was the only way that I could get company for my thoughts and persuade the grown-ups to talk, however insincerely, on the same subject. The session opened of course with a little lecture from Aunt Catherine about the folly of the whole thing. Then the curtains were drawn and Uncle Tom began. His personality and prestige added to the

effect, for he was tall and bony and we held him in awe. He told the old stories about midnight coaches, about grinning lift-men who had been seen in a dream the night before, about grey monks who had passed people on the stairs and figures standing at midnight by one's bed; and they all to me had the same face.

The wind rose rapidly in accompaniment to his tales, and our feelings of horror were already far outstripping the merits of his invention, when a really terrible thing happened. A gust of wind tore open the casement and at the same time the bell in the tower gave a jerky ring. There was no need to tell us any more stories. Our hearts were tight with presentiment. Its variable sound came and went with the gusts even after the window was tightly closed again. It was not like a bell rung on purpose, but a bell evilly twitching on its own.

'This is quite intolerable,' said Aunt Catherine. 'No one will sleep a wink tonight if that goes on.'

'Don't get in a fuss,' said Uncle; 'I'll go and take out the clapper. Nothing could be simpler. Now, boys, off to bed.'

Up we went perforce, keeping close together, and clustered at our bedroom window to see him do this act of bravery. He seemed to waste hours talking to Aunt in the hall while we waited upstairs and listened to that vibrating shudder from the bell, the irregularity of which made it even more fraying to the nerves. The shadows under the yard walls were peopled for me with precise terror, and so was the room at my back. The key-hole howled too, and the wind in the chimney buffeted hollowly. At last we saw Uncle Tom come out into the light from the back door, and go down the yard where we could only by straining keep him in sight. Shadows swallowed him up and we heard the barn door slam behind him. We fixed our eyes on the outline of the bell tower, and again it seemed an age before we thought we could distinguish his head, shoulders and arms waving against the sky.

'There he is,' said John, in a whisper. Uncle had seized the bell and the clanging stopped; but a moment later we heard him yell with the whole force of his great lungs, and his body disappeared down the man-hole. The bell had stopped, but the wind still blew and it was hard to tell where sounds came from. Robert thought he heard a dog-fight going on somewhere. But Uncle Tom didn't come back. Time seemed too short now. We imagined how long it would be before he would appear, then doubled it, trebled it, and began again.

At last Aunt Catherine came out and shouted for him, ran half-way down the yard and shouted again. The maid came out too, and presently the yard was full of people with lamps and flash-lights. They went into the barn after Aunt Catherine, and came staggering out carrying someone towards the house. We were seized with shame and undressed as quickly as we could, jumping into our beds. But Robert went on to the landing and called down the stairs to ask what had happened.

'Go to bed, boys, and for the Lord's sake keep quiet and keep out of the way,' said a woman neighbour. 'Your uncle has had a nasty accident.'

And then we heard the horrible mad banshee sound of the maid having hysterics in the kitchen.

YI CHANG AND THE HAUNTED HOUSE

Eleanore M. Jewett

Yi Chang lived in the city of Seoul. He was very poor, very lazy, and very friendly. Because he was lazy he did little work, earned less money, and rarely had shelter to cover his head. Because he was friendly he found many to wish him well, to talk to him of this and that, and to give him advice as to where he might get him a meal now and then, without too much effort. In short, he was not so poor in heart as he was in bodily possessions. He would have liked very much to have a house of his own, no matter how small and shabby, and was always looking about to see if he could find some tumble-down hut that he could get for little or nothing.

'Now if you were willing to live in a haunted house,' said a friend of his one day, 'I know of one to be had for the taking.'

Yi Chang looked doubtful, then grinned. 'Why not?' said he. 'I like company. Perhaps a ghost or two would cheer me up on a lonely winter evening. Where is it, this haunted house of which you speak?'

After getting his directions, Yi Chang went to see the place. It stood on a little-travelled road in a section of Seoul called Ink Town at the foot of South Mountain. When he made enquiries about it people shook their heads and clicked their tongues. An old house, rather fine in its day and doubtless still in good repair, they said, but for many years it had been empty. Yes, haunted, without question, but why or by what man-

ner of spirit none knew. Indeed no one had been fool-
hardy enough to enter the grounds, let alone the house,
for as many years back as could be remembered. They
strongly advised Yi Chang to have nothing to do with
it.

He looked at the place long and questioningly from
across the road. Over the weather-stained wall that surrounded it he could see the roof of the house, a tile
roof, not one made of grass and thatch like a poor man's
dwelling. The corners of it turned up at a proper angle,
pagoda fashion, which should make it proof against in-
vading evil spirits. He crossed the road and, after a
moment's hesitation, pushed open a gate of the wall
and approached the building. A wide clay-floored
porch, or matang, extended across the front. Yi Chang
skirted it and made his way through a tangle of weeds
and garden plants run riot, to the back. There he found
the usual kitchen court with a furnace which seemed to
be in good condition. There were ample grates and
shelves for cooking, and heat evidently had been piped
through flues under the floors to keep the house warm
in winter.

Yi Chang sighed with satisfaction. Truly, he thought,
any man would be more than fortunate to live in such
a place. Then he stepped up from the kitchen court
into the house itself, there being nothing to prevent
him, and looked around. Dust lay thick upon the floor,
so thick and so completely untracked that he decided
no living feet could have passed over it for years. There
were a few bowls and eating utensils lying about, also
grey with dust, and spiderwebs hung in the corners of
the windows. His courage ebbed a little but he moved
slowly across the floor, being as careful as if the stirring
up of the dust and breaking of the cobwebs might rouse
the dead. Perhaps it might! Ghosts might indeed be
sleeping at that moment in the silent rooms and pas-

sages beyond. Yi Chang decided he would not explore farther for the present. It would be much pleasanter to have someone with him. Then a thought struck him. Hu and Haw, his two older brothers, lived in a little village not very far from Seoul. They were strong and bold, although a little stupid, perhaps. Why not get them to join him, help him clean up the place—or better, clean it up for him—and stay with him until he found out a little more about the hauntings? He would tell them just enough to stir their interest and curiosity, not enough to frighten them.

Yi Chang put his thought speedily into action, and soon Hu and Haw, burly country fellows, had joined him and were ready to begin the process of cleaning. Together they went through the whole house. There was nothing unusual to be seen; every room was bare of all furnishings and thick with untracked dust. The paper partitions were whole and the doors slid easily—all except one. In the section of the house customarily reserved for the men of the family, there was one room they could not enter. Curiosity mounted in the three of them as they stood outside that tightly closed door.

At length Hu took a knife from his belt. 'Why not thrust through the wall here beside the door? It would be simple enough to make a small peep hole, barely visible.'

'Very well,' agreed Yi Chang, after a moment's hesitation, for by now he considered himself the owner of the place. 'A very small hole will do no harm.'

An opening was accordingly made, and Hu, Haw, and Yi Chang looked through it in turn and then exchanged puzzled glances.

'A harp with broken strings, a pair of worn shoes, some sticks, an old kettle, and a broken sieve,' Haw counted off. 'Surely no one in his senses would carefully lock up such rubbish!'

'Let us break in the door,' suggested Hu, preparing at once to do so.

But Yi Chang held him back. 'Not so fast, brother,' said he. 'Someone has put those things there, someone to whom they mean something. It is best to leave them alone. I shall have plenty of rooms without this one.'

So they set about cleaning the house, or rather Hu and Haw cleaned while Yi Chang gave directions and talked in a friendly and affectionate manner. All day they were busy, and only towards sundown did they lay aside their cloths and cleaning sticks. Yi Chang declared he was tired and the other two were willing enough to stop work and go out on the matang. They would rest a bit and eat the food they had brought with them.

But when they had stepped out on the porch, they started back in astonishment. Two large dogs lay sleeping at either end of it. One was tan and the other as black at midnight. Hu and Haw approached the tan dog cautiously while Yi Chang watched. They laid their hands upon the creature, gently at first, and then more roughly. It did not stir.

'Warm?' asked Yi Chang.

Hu nodded.

'I thought maybe they were dead.' He ventured a gentle kick at the black dog. No sign of life except the even motion of his sides as he breathed.

The three looked at each other in growing wonder.

'What *are* they?' questioned Hu. 'Surely not natural beasts!'

'Where did they come from? And how did they get in? I closed the gate behind us. I don't like it!' Haw said uneasily.

'It *is* strange—very strange,' Yi Chang agreed, 'but at least they seem harmless. Let them lie.'

Hu and Haw rather reluctantly settled themselves on the clay floor of the porch as far from the dogs as possible. It had been a warm day and the cool of the evening was pleasant. After they had eaten they stretched out and were soon asleep.

Yi Chang sat where he could keep an eye on the animals, for, in spite of his confident words, he was uneasy about them. Long after his two brothers had fallen asleep he watched. Nothing happened, however, and at last he too fell into a doze.

He was aroused by the sound of pattering steps on the clay flooring. By the light of a bright moon that was now riding the skies he could see the two dogs, who had left their stations, restlessly pacing back and forth, sniffing the air, then nosing the ground, as if seeking for a scent.

A gong from a distant temple rang the hour. Midnight. Immediately the dogs, facing the moon, began to bay drearily. The sound wakened Hu and Haw who, with stifled screams of alarm, would have made off had not Yi Chang grasped them, one with each hand.

'Idiots!' he hissed as they wrenched themselves free. 'Cowards! What are you afraid of? Two dogs baying at the moon?'

Rather shamefaced, the two turned back.

'See, they are paying no attention whatever to us! Let us get into the shadows and watch,' Yi Chang suggested.

The three backed into a corner of the porch into which the light of the moon did not penetrate.

Almost at once the howling of the dogs changed to sharp, delighted barks of welcome and they began jumping about, wagging their tails and showing every sign of happy greeting to a loved master. And there on the centre of the porch, his slender white hands caressing their heads, stood a strange figure. It was a little old gentleman dressed in ceremonial costume; a long white garment of rich silk, with flowing sleeves, the collar cut according to the careful usage of men of high social standing. On his head was the customary horsehair hat with a narrow crown cut off like a truncated pyramid. The stem of the long curved pipe in his mouth showed white in the moonlight.

How he had got onto the porch without the three seeing him they could not imagine. Perhaps the moon had slipped under a cloud, but it was very clear and bright at that moment and they noticed that neither man nor dogs, standing in the full light of it, cast any shadow.

The old gentleman now entered the house and the dogs returned to their posts at either end of the veranda.

It took not a little urging and reassuring on the part of Yi Chang to persuade his brothers to follow him indoors and see what their curious visitor might be doing. Finally they agreed, keeping Yi Chang well ahead of them and being ready to flee at the slightest hint of danger.

They had no light save that of the moon shining in through windows and doors. Corners and inner passageways were black and threatening. The three tiptoed silently from room to room, pausing often to listen. Not a sound broke the stillness. All doors were open as they had left them after cleaning the place, and the heavy paper partitions separating the rooms gave no hint of light or motion behind them, at least until they reached the locked room.

Hu, Haw, and Yi Chang stood motionless, scarcely breathing. It was not a sound exactly but a sense of motion, the barest possible whisper and stir, that issued from that closed and mysterious apartment. Through the paper walls they became aware of a faint luminousness which was not really light but a slight thinning of the heavy dark. The three drew closer together, trembling.

The light from within grew brighter and suddenly chords of music, weird, high, exciting, burst forth— dance music! The shuffling of a pair of shoes could be heard, then laughter and gay voices, the rattling of sticks, the hollow tones of a kettle struck as if it were a drum, and dominating the rhythm the sweet, vibrant chords of a harp.

Yi Chang, full of wonder, left the other two and crept noiselessly to the hole Hu had pierced in the wall beside the sliding bamboo doors. He was just about to put his eye to it when a sword blade was shot through from within—a blue steel blade that glittered with unearthly light. Yi Ching barely avoided it by a sudden jump to one side.

Then the three fled in panic, never minding the clatter they made as they rushed through the house to the clay porch and from that to the gate of the wall and out into the street.

The next morning they consulted together. Hu and Haw were for returning to their home farm without delay. They'd had enough, said they, of Seoul in general and of that evil, haunted house in particular. But Yi Chang was not satisfied. Now, in the broad daylight, the house and grounds looked ordinary enough with no sign of anything unusual.

'We spent yesterday there safely,' he said to his uneasy brothers. 'Why not go through the house once again and see whether those ghostly revellers have left anything interesting behind them?'

Rather unwillingly Hu and Haw agreed. The house, when they had entered it, showed the effects of their cleaning but otherwise was as empty and harmless-looking as could be imagined.

When they reached the locked room Yi Chang very cautiously put his eye to the peep hole. Everything was exactly as it had been before. Harp, sticks, kettle, shoes, sieve, were standing just where they had been and were thick with dust. Yi Chang drew back; the other two looked through into the room, then questioningly at each other.

Hu had an idea. 'Look you,' said he, speaking in a whisper, as if afraid unseen creatures might be listening. 'I have often heard it said that the way to drive off ghosts and evil spirits is to burn the objects that they use.'

'Ai!' exclaimed Haw, 'the very thing! Let us break through into this haunted room, gather up the articles there, and burn them out in the garden.'

Yi Chang hesitated but finally nodded a reluctant consent.

It was easy enough to break the heavy paper walls. The three, being uneasy and fearful, worked with speed and soon had the oddly assorted contents of the room piled in the garden with dry leaves and twigs under and over them, ready for a light.

But Yi Chang was worried and unhappy. He watched with a long face and mournful eyes as the fire caught and began to lick the harp. Suddenly he leaped into the blaze and pulled it out. While the other two gaped in amazement he stamped and beat upon the flames, at the same time seizing one object after another and throwing it to safety.

'By the soul of my maternal ancestor,' cried Haw, 'what are you doing?'

And as Yi Chang made no answer, Hu pulled at his sleeve. 'Don't you know we are doing the only thing that will rid your house of ghosts and goblins?'

Yi Chang stopped stamping out the blaze, which was nearly smothered, and brushed the smoke and ashes from his clothing before he answered. 'That is just it,' he said. 'This house is no more mine than *theirs*, whoever they are. And besides, they sound like very gay

company. Why should I destroy their simple possessions and so spoil their festivities?'

'I suppose you may even be minded to join them at
some ghostly revel!' said Haw sarcastically.

'Until they hang you upside down in a tree or beat
you to death or bury you in a deserted tomb! Ghosts
and goblins do such things, you know!' Hu snorted in
disgust as he spoke.

Yi Chang merely shrugged his shoulders and grinned.

'Very well,' said Haw, 'we will leave you to your
haunted house and ghostly company. Come, Hu, let us
return to our peaceful home in the country!'

With that, the two brothers Hu and Haw went off
without another word.

As for Yi Chang, he gathered up the broken-stringed
harp, the worn shoes, the kettle, the sticks, and the sieve
and returned them to the room from which they had
been taken. With much care he mended the torn wall,
even patching up the peep hole so that he would have
no further temptation to pry. The next day he settled
himself in the haunted house.

Weeks passed, months, a year. Then Hu and Haw,
unable to bear their curiosity any longer, returned to
Seoul and betook themselves to Ink Town at the foot
of South Mountain. They intended to find out about
their brother before telling him of their arrival and so
sought out neighbours secretly to ask about him.

'Yes, oh yes, the lad Yi Chang is still living in the
haunted house,' said one.

'And very happy and prosperous he seems,' said another.

'Always ready with a smile or a friendly nod whenever he sees any of us,' said a third. 'Friendly—that's
what he is. One cannot help liking him though he
must be an odd one, the way he goes on living over
yonder.'

'Maybe the house is not haunted any more?' suggested Hu.

The three neighbours smiled and winked knowingly at each other. 'There is no maybe about it. It is still haunted!' said the first with authority. But beyond that no one would say anything.

Hu and Haw hesitated and consulted together and decided they would investigate further. So, shortly before midnight, they were again on the road outside their brother's house, watching, listening, and wondering.

The temple gong struck the hour. Immediately they heard the baying of dogs beyond the wall, then welcoming barks. Very cautiously they stepped inside the gate. The house was in total darkness and silence. They waited breathlessly. In a few moments a light glowed from the house, music sounded, laughter, and the chattering of voices. The shuffle of dancing feet kept time to the rhythmic, highly accented music in which the mellow tones of the harp could be heard. It seemed as if the whole house must be shaken with it. The two, in a panic, rushed for the gate in the wall, only to find themselves face to face with Yi Chang.

'Well, my brothers,' said he, 'have you come to pay me a visit?'

'N-n-no,' stammered Hu, 'not exactly.'

'We—we—just happened to be passing,' added Haw, edging closer to the gate.

'And you must leave so soon?' Yi Chang smiled and then laughed. 'I thought I might persuade you to join me and my companions in our festivity tonight.'

'Your companions?' Hu repeated in awe. 'Then you —you—have really made friends with them? You are not afraid?'

'No, not at all,' said Yi Chang. 'Why should one be afraid of friends?'

'But—who *are* they?' whispered Haw. '*What* are they?'

Yi Chang shrugged his shoulders and answered indifferently. 'I do not really know, but does it matter? They are friends. Come! I will make you acquainted with them!'

But Hu and Haw would not be persuaded. Another look at the house with its one glowing window and its strange, unearthly music growing wilder every moment was enough for them. They bade Yi Chang farewell and hurried away. Behind them they heard their brother's step on the matang floor, the excited, happy barking of two dogs greeting him, and many thin, faint voices shouting welcome.

After they had walked for a long time in silence through the deserted streets of Seoul, Hu said, 'He is a very friendly person, our brother Yi Chang.'

'Yes,' agreed Haw thoughtfully. 'And it is a good thing to be friendly; one can see that—friendly with everybody.'

'Even with ghosts?' Hu's voice sounded a little doubtful but Haw spoke with conviction.

'Even with ghosts!'

SPOOKS OF THE VALLEY

Louis C. Jones

The boys were working intently on the tail assembly of the model transport plane. Joe was holding the small piece of balsa wood neatly in place while Pete carefully spread the glue along the crevice. It was well after bedtime, for Pete's folks, when they went out, had told the boys to go upstairs at eight-thirty, and now the clock was striking nine. But the problem of the tail was a tough one and could hardly be left for tomorrow. Besides, Joe didn't come to spend the night very often. When they heard the first step on the top stair they hardly noticed it. At the second step Pete spoke up sharply, but without raising his eyes from their task.

'Sis, you get on back to bed. You know what Mom told you. You're gonna get in trouble.'

The footsteps kept coming slowly down the stairs just as he rather expected they would, young sisters being what they are. It wasn't the weight on the steps that made him turn, for that was light enough, but Sister never came down a pair of stairs slowly in her life. And if it wasn't Carol, who was it? This took a few seconds, especially since Pete's mind really wasn't on the stairs but on the model. It wasn't until Joe said, 'Okay now,' and put the tube of glue down, that Pete turned around.

Never before had he seen the man who stood there —tall and gaunt, with tanned, knotty hands and a weary stoop to his shoulders. His clothes were ragged and strangely out of date. Pete wasn't scared, just surprised. You couldn't really be scared of a face like this man's. It was an interesting face, with kind, sad lines around the mouth and the grey eyes. It looked like a face that had seen a lot of things, and the expression of the eyes made you ponder. Pete was still gaping when Joe spoke.

'Well, hello, George. So you really came up, did you?'

'Yeah,' the man said, 'I figured you two would be alone tonight so I kind of hung around outside until Pete's folks went away. Then I just wandered in and looked around until I found you.'

'Who is this guy?' Pete asked, still surprised not to see his sister.

'This is George, Pete. I told you about George. I told you all about him on the bus the other day.'

'You mean,' said Pete, 'that you weren't kidding? I thought you made all that up.'

'Pete, you know I never make things up. I'm not always having crazy ideas like you. George, this is Pete.'

'Pete, I'm glad to meet you. I'm mighty glad to meet you, 'cause I think you can help me,' said George in a hopeful voice.

'Gee, I'd like to help you, George,' said Pete. 'That is—I guess I would. Are you really—I mean, is it like Joe told me? Aren't you——?'

'Well, now, Pete, I don't know. I don't know just what Joe told you. If he told you how I used to peddle tin all through this section, and how this was the last farm I ever stopped at, and how I'm needing your help now—I guess he told you right. You see, Pete, the way it is, I can't rest. I got this thing on my mind all the time, and that way you don't get any rest. People ought not to do things like that, and it was a long time ago, of course, and somebody who lives here now has got to make it right. I tried to get to your old man, and I tried

103

to get to your mom, but they couldn't hear me and they couldn't see me. I figured maybe you were the only one I could talk to.'

'Well, gee, George, I guess we can help you if it isn't too hard to do. Do we have to do it tonight?'

'Well,' said George, 'it would be kind of nice if you could. This business is sort of delicate, but there's a good moon out, and though I don't want to get you in trouble, it will be quite a spell before your folks get back.'

He seemed so earnest and hopeful about it that the boys felt they really had to help.

'How do we start?' asked Joe.

'All you got to do, boys, is this. You go out to that big woodpile—the old woodpile in the back of the barn——'

'We haven't touched that woodpile since we moved here four years ago,' broke in Pete. 'Pop cut down so many trees and sawed 'em up for firewood that we just haven't had to use that wood out behind the barn.'

'I know that, son,' said George, 'and nobody else has touched that woodpile. Some of that wood's been there ten years, and before that they kept putting fresh wood on every winter, so that nobody's been down to the bottom of that pile since 1853. But all I want you boys to do is go down to the far end of that pile and tear it to pieces. Get right down to the ground and then start digging until you come to the place where my tin is buried. Won't be much now—just a few pieces of rust—but then you'll know you're in the right spot and you keep digging down below that. Then you come to the important thing. . . .'

Pete was listening intently to every word George said, and then suddenly he realised that something weird and wonderful was happening. George was disappearing. It was not that he was going away—it's just that

when he finished the sentence, he wasn't there. First
there had been three of them and now there were only
two.

'Whillikers!' said Pete, 'I'd somehow forgotten all
about his being dead.'

Pete ran upstairs and looked in to see if his brother
and sister were asleep. They certainly were, all right.
Carol was snoring happily to herself and Davie was
hugging his little old bear for dear life. Then Pete got
some mittens and a couple of sweaters, because the
October air was cold. Both boys walked out the back
door and down behind the barn where the full moon
shone cold and clear on the old woodpile, six feet high
and four cord wide.

The wood was dry and light, and they started at the
top and threw it off the cord so it fell every which way
in the grass. After a little bit Joe was puffing and Pete
had stopped to sit down and rest himself.

'This isn't easy!' Pete said slowly.

'But we gotta do it. I promised George that first
night I met him.'

'How'd you get mixed up in this, Joe?'

'It was like I told you—that calf Pa gave me got her
foot caught in a stanchion. I heard her bellowing and
went down to the barn along about nine o'clock to get
it loose. Coming back, I saw lights in the old Staats
house. I knew the Staatses weren't there, and down the
little road between our house and theirs I saw George
pacing up and down. 'Course I didn't know he was a
—I mean, I thought he was just a man. I didn't see any
reason to be scared of him, so I says "Hello" and he says
"Hello, you're Joe, aren't you?" And I says, "Yep, I'm
Joe. I never saw you around before." So he says, "No,
but I been watching you. Sometimes I see you down
here and sometimes I see you visitin' up to your friend

Pete's." So I says, "Do you know Pete?" And he says, "Nope, but I wish I did. He's about the only one could really help me." "What's the matter?" I says to him, and he comes back with "What I got, the trouble with me, is hard to say. I'm not like you. I been dead, you know, 'most a hundred years." Well, when he said it like that, Pete, I could have jumped. We see 'em around, of course. Especially at night around the Staats place where they like to come—they have parties down there sometimes. But I never talked to one, 'specially not about being a ghost. You might say he was just matter of fact about it. Like I'd say, "I'm a boy." That's the way he said it.'

Pete was quiet for a minute. Then he said, 'I think I would have been scared.'

'You weren't scared tonight when George came in. The dead seem so natural, don't they?'

There was a long silence then. Somewhere a lone bird chirped just a little. Mr Ostrander's cow complained in the next field. It was awful quiet. After a bit the boys got up and began pulling down the pile again. they were halfway done now. Their hands were getting tired and they were slowing down. After a while they took another spell of sitting, and Pete said, 'When did he tell you, exactly, about this?'

'It was that same night after I had gone to bed. George came into the room and sat down and told me. It seems that the year this all happened, he was carrying around all the money he had saved up for five years. He was gonna open a little store down in Hudson or Catskill or someplace. He didn't know anybody to take care of the money for him and he didn't trust banks, so he had it all wadded up in big bills in his pants' pocket. It came along towards winter and he had pretty well sold out everything he had. When he started out he had had a horse and cart piled up with tin—pots, pans, and stuff. He was down to four or five pans, and the week before he had had a chance to sell his horse and cart for a good price. He wasn't going to need them when he opened up his store so he grabbed the chance and sold out.

'Well, he came to your house along about dusk one night and some new folks had bought the place. There was a man and a woman with the meanest hired man he had ever seen in his life—a great burly fellow with hairy arms, and his teeth stuck out of the corners like a dog. George asked them could he stay there that night. All he wanted was a place to lay his blanket. They said he could sleep on the floor up in the hired man's room.'

'That must be my room now, isn't it?' asked Pete, trying to get a word in edgewise.

'That's the way I figure it. Anyway, this hired man didn't like the idea, was mighty crabby about it.

'When they were getting undressed George suddenly sneezed and he pulled his handkerchief out and this big wad of bills came with it. The fellow saw the bills and didn't say much, but after George had got to sleep he had this dream about not being able to breathe. Just as he was waking up, he opened his eyes, and the moonlight was coming right on the face of this great big fellow who was choking the very life out of him. Well, sir, he was dead before he knew it.

'Then he stayed around while the hired man picked up his body and very carefully came down those back stairs from your bedroom, down through the kitchen, out in back where this woodpile is—right here where we're sitting. And George says first he took the wood down just like we've done now. Then he dug a grave under where the woodpile had been, putting the dirt into bushel baskets. Then he buried George and put the tin that was left on top, covered it over with dirt

107

and piled up the wood again the way it had been. Then he took the dirt that was left and spread it all over the garden. The next morning he just told the folks that the tin man had left at the crack of dawn.'

Maybe it was the cold, maybe it was a stray owl that was hooting out in the pine trees, maybe it was the funny shadows that passed over the moon—but Pete sat on the woodpile shivering.

'Look, Joe, what do you say we do this some other time? I'm not so sure I want to get mixed up in this.'

'You wouldn't let me down now, would you?' came a third voice from the darkness. And there was George, standing there looking at him, sad as he could be.

'Pete, my boy, you don't know what it is to have your body buried off in a forsaken spot like the bottom of a woodpile. A man likes to feel he's buried with people. You don't have to have a fancy monument, but the place for a dead man is in a cemetery, and I can't rest like a man ought to until my bones are taken out of this place and put where they belong.'

'What about this hired man, George?' Pete's voice was small and sort of sick sounding.

'Oh, him!' George answered. 'It didn't take me long to handle him. Two days after he'd killed me, he ran away from here, and I followed him. He went out and walked along the railroad track. About two miles from here, just beyond Van Hoesen, a train came pounding down the line and he stepped off the track, but not quite far enough. I gave him a little shove and that was the end of him. It's a bad thing to have a dead man mad at you. It's a worse thing to steal a dead man's money—'specially if it's every cent he's saved for six hard years. I tell you, Pete, I never hurt a single soul as long as I was alive, but he was a bummer and I fixed him in my own time.'

Pete's worry wasn't quite caught up.

'He isn't still around by any chance?' he asked apprehensively.

'I never saw him,' said George. 'He never comes down with the others to the Staats place when we have our meetings. No, I never saw him again.'

After a pause, he said, 'Now what do you say, boys —let's get this done. There isn't much time, you know, before your folks get back.'

They worked hard for a few minutes and then another few and before they knew it, sure enough, they were down to the bare ground. Pete disappeared and came back with a spade and a shovel—and while George watched, they dug.

Now this was really hard work and they began to sweat and pant. Just as it seemed an endless job, there was a scraping noise and something more than stone was in the dirt. When they picked it up, it was the handle of a skillet. George remembered it.

'A first-rate piece of merchandise.' That's what he said of it. But now there was just a handle—the rest had rusted away. But there were other pieces of metal and the boys kept digging.

'Take it easy now. I think you're getting close,' George cautioned. And, sure enough, pretty soon a bone like the upper part of a man's arm lay in the dirt. Pete got a bushel basket and put it in very gently. Joe kept digging and soon they found another. And another. Finally the skull—full of dirt and worms, but clean as it could be once you knocked the soil away. As George watched them carefully putting each piece in the basket, he spoke softly:

'You're very kind to me, boys. Very thoughtful young men you are.'

Pretty soon Joe asked him, 'Have we got it all there now? Seems like we've picked a couple of hundred bones out of the dirt. They're hard to see, you know, even in the moonlight.'

'I think there's a hand missing, boys. It feels to me that way. I don't feel you've got my other hand.'

'Do you have any idea where it would be?' Joe asked.

'Try right there,' said George and pointed.

They dug a little more and pretty soon they found the bones as though they had been all clenched together and the boys picked them up in a couple of handfuls. They took the basket and hid it in the haymow in the barn and then came back to fill the hole in just as fast as they could move. Then they piled up the wood again as best they could. Fortunately, that was a part of the farm where almost no one ever came, so its chance of being seen was pretty small. The midnight express went screaming down the B. & A. tracks a mile away about the time the boys had piled the last stick in place.

The past half hour Pete had been getting nervous because he knew that it was almost time for his folks to be coming home and if he weren't in bed asleep, they'd make an awful squawk. And if they knew what he had been up to, there was no telling what would happen. Every time a car light came up the road he would look over his shoulder at it.

'What's the matter, Pete?' George asked. 'You ain't still worrying about that hired man, are you?'

'No, I was more worried about my old man than your hired man. It's about time they're comin' home.'

'Oh, them,' said George, 'don't worry about them. I had one of my friends in town stick a nail in your father's tyre, just so he wouldn't hurry home too fast. I don't think he'll be here for a spell yet. And, boys, I want to say how grateful I am to you, but there's one other little matter. Where are you going to rebury me?'

'Well,' said Joe, 'I thought we'd take you down to that old burying ground outside the Staats place. It would be near the house down there and handy for your parties.'

'That's fine,' said George, 'that's fine. Now, when?' There was persistence in his tone.

'Well,' said Pete, 'I'm going down to Joe's to spend Saturday night and if you wouldn't mind my putting the bones in a bag, I could take them down on my bike when I go. Then we could fix it up for you some time over the weekend.'

'Boys, that's just fine. That's just fine. Down there I'll be real happy. If there's anything I can ever do for you, you let me know.'

'It's okay,' said Joe, 'we're glad to help you out.'

'Would you— some time——' broke off Pete, not knowing how to go on.

'What, son? Anything at all.'

'Saturday, mebbe, would you tell us more about— about being dead? And about some of the ghosts—the other ghosts, I mean.'

'Why not? I'll tell you all I know—and what I don't know ain't worth knowin'.' And for the first time George grinned at them. 'You bury me the way I ought to be, and then Saturday we'll get together. How's that?' They were about to answer him, but George had disappeared once more.

Right after breakfast on Saturday Pete fed the chickens and before his mother quite realised it, he was off on his bike for Joe's house. In the basket on his handle bars was a grain bag, neatly folded. It made an irregular package but it weighed so little that he barely realised it was there. Best of all, he had been able to hide it up by the trees at the north end of his farm the night before, so that in the morning he could pick it up without the endless questions that grown-ups are for ever asking a boy.

Pete lived two miles or more back from the Hudson, high above the river. He pedalled along rapidly, finally coming to the airport road which dropped down to the river road, past Citizen Genet's old house. As he swung down the hill, bracing himself against the pull of the brakes, he caught the long view of the river with Albany to the right, its hillside towers against the sky, then far to the left the Castleton bridge carrying the freight trains over the cut-off. When he reached the river road he turned left for a mile, then took a side road leading to the river.

Joe lived on an island, separated from the mainland by a longish bridge. Before the river was deepened it was more of an island, but even now during the spring floods sometimes they were cut off from the mainland. As Pete pumped his bike up over the New York Central tracks he could see the farm buildings ahead of him, the ancient barns and the farmhouse made over and modernised but really the same house that had been there for nearly two centuries.

'Hi, Joeyeeee.' It made a crazy sound as Pete called it.

But back from the barn came 'Hiyi, Pete.' And he came running.

Five minutes later the two boys were walking rapidly down the little grass-covered wagon track that led to the south end of the island and the old Staats house with its aged cemetery. Each carried a shovel over his shoulder and the bag of bones between them, not because it was heavy, but to share the responsibility.

'George was here last night,' said Joe casually.

'Yeah?'

'He told me just where he wants them buried. Over near old Jakob Staats in the far corner. Says the old man was a good customer of his and a good friend. And besides, no one will notice a new grave there.'

By now they had come to the gateway of the little family burying ground with its headstones that told the story of a family that are said to have come to the Hudson Valley some time before 1640 and had always lived on that land. The boys found Jakob's grave off in a far corner, just as George had told Joe they would, and they began to dig. It was easy going, for the soil was sandy.

'How deep do you think we ought to go?' Pete asked when they were down a couple of feet.

'Six feet is the customary depth,' said a voice that made them jump halfway out of their skins.

'Holy Moses, George! I wish you wouldn't scare us so,' scolded Joe.

'I thought you had to wait till night, George. Can you come around any—Hey, George, where are you?' Pete was bewildered, for, close as the voice was, there was no George to be seen.

'Pete, my friend,' the old man said, 'your notions about us dead are way out of date. Any time of day or night, that's us. Sometimes we "show" and sometimes we don't; that's up to us. Look!'

And sure enough, after a second or two there he was, as real as a tree. Then he roared with laughter, slapping his thigh, as he saw the look on the boys' faces. 'There are a lot of silly notions going around about us. Chain rattling, for instance. Almost nobody, that is, no *dead* body, rattles chains, that I know of. And water! They tell you we can't cross water. Fiddle-faddle! How would the whole bunch of us get to an *island* for our meetings and parties, down here at the Staats house, if we couldn't cross water? As a matter of fact, we can do almost anything we could when we were alive. More things, really. Couldn't disappear when I was alive.' And with that he wasn't there any more, just the sound of his laugh as the boys stared at the air where he had been.

'George is feeling a lot more cheerful, isn't he?' Pete observed.

'Told me he felt like a new spirit since we dug him up,' Joe said. 'He's much more fun than he was.'

They dug for a spell, thinking over what they had heard, thinking, too, about the fact that George was there by them, watching. They figured the hole didn't have to be very long or wide. First one would get down and work awhile, then the other. They did a lot of resting, but not even Joe was talking much. The deeper they went, the harder going it was. When Pete was waist-deep he said, 'George, that isn't six feet, but how about it? Don't you think that's deep enough?'

'We-ell, lads, each of you do six more shovelfuls and we'll call it a day. But if we don't get it right now, I'll have trouble later. Get it right and I can rest easy till Judgment Day.'

'Won't we be seeing you any more after this, George?'

'Today and tonight. Then I'm going to be leaving for good, Joey, me lad. No sense hanging around when things are the way they ought to be. When everything is settled up and there are no loose ends, a man can rest. If his conscience is clear, of course.'

'Does that really make a difference?' asked Pete.

'Does it! I could tell you stories about friends of mine who will *never* get straightened out, because of the things they can't forget, things that weigh on their minds and will for all eternity.'

'You wouldn't want to tell us, would you, George? We got nothing much to do today, have we, Pete?'

'Not a thing, Joe, and this is our last chance, George. If we do ten shovels apiece deeper, instead of six, would you tell us?'

'You boys get them bones buried right as rain and I'll have some time for you. We could go up by the old light and watch the river, so's I can always have the look of it in my mind. Don't know as I could spend a better day.'

The boys did twenty shovels apiece till they were shoulder deep. Then they put some pine boughs in the bottom of the grave and laid the bones out, more or less the way they ought to have lain, only snugger. There

were a lot of odds and ends they couldn't recognise, but they put the head at the top, and the arms along the sides, the ribs in the middle, then the legs. The odds and ends they laid neatly in the centre. George's voice kept saying how pleased he was, and how grateful. Then they put some more pine boughs over the lot of them and began filling in.

'Do you need any words said, George?' asked Joe.

'Well, now, boy, that's real nice of you to remember. I reckon it would make it more official and there sure weren't any words said last time, only a few cuss words. You might each think a little prayer or something.'

'Does it matter what kind, George? I'm Catholic and Pete here is some kind of Protestant——'

'Presbyterian,' corrected Pete.

'You fellers each say one of your own kind and that'll do fine. I didn't get around to go to much of any church in the old days, so the brand won't matter. You might say 'em silent-like. That'll do first rate.'

So the boys said a prayer apiece and when they raised their heads they looked over to the place where the voice had been coming from. Only now George was standing there again and his face was one great smile. 'That sure was mighty right and nice.'

After that it didn't take them very long to finish the job. They were agreed that it would be better not to put any stones or marker over the spot, since, in the summertime, the Staats family came back once in a while to the burying ground and they might wonder about a new grave. Instead they pulled some vines over the place and piled up some leaves that were blown into a corner. Then they stood back a way and found that they had done a good job of concealment.

'Let's go ask my mother for some sandwiches and tell her we're going up to the other end of the island to explore. Will you come, George?'

'Today I'll do whatever you lads want me to.'

'We want to hear about your friends, the ones who can't rest on account of their consciences,' Pete said.

THE WATER WOMAN AND HER LOVER

It's an old Essequibo tale they used to tell in whispers. But even as they whispered the tale they were afraid the wind might blow their whisperings into the river where the water woman lived. They were afraid the water woman might hear their whisperings and return to haunt them as she had haunted her lover.

It's a strange story. Here it is from the beginning:

There was an old koker near Parika, through which water passed to and from the Essequibo river, for drainage of the lands in the area. On moonlit nights a naked woman was often seen sitting near the koker, with her back to the road and her face to the river.

She was a fair-skinned woman, and she had long, black, shiny hair rolling over her shoulders and down her back. Below her waist she was like a fish. When the moon was bright, especially at full-moon time, you could see her sitting on the koker, combing her long, black, shiny hair. You could see very dimly just a part of her face—a side view. But you stepped nearer to get a closer look she would disappear. Without even turning her head to see who was coming, she would plunge into the river with a splash and vanish. They called her Water Mama.

People used to come from Salem, Tuschen, Naamryck and other parts of the east bank of the Essequibo river to see this mysterious creature. They would wait in the bush or near the koker from early morning, and watch to see her rise from the river. But no matter how closely they watched, they would never see her when she came from the water. For a long time they would wait, and watch the koker bathed in moonlight. Then suddenly, as if she had sprung from nowhere, the water woman would appear sitting near the koker, completely naked, facing the river, and combing her long, black hair.

There was a strong belief among the villagers in the area that riches would come to anyone who found Water Mama's comb, or a lock of her hair. So they used to stay awake all night at the koker, and then early in the morning, even before the sun rose, they would search around where she had sat combing her hair. But they never found anything. Only the water that had drained off her body remained behind—and also a strong fishy smell.

The old people said that after looking at Water Mama or searching near the koker for her hair and her comb, you were always left feeling haunted and afraid. They told stories of people found sleeping, as if in a trance, while walking away from the koker. They warned that if a man watched her too long, and searched for her hair and her comb too often, he would dream about her. And if the man loved her and she loved him, she would haunt him in his dreams. And that would be the end of him, they said, because she was a creature of the devil. These warnings did not frighten the younger and more adventurous men from the villages around. They kept coming from near and far to gaze at Water Mama. After watching her and searching for her hair and her comb, they always had that haunted, fearful feeling. And many mornings, even as they walked away from the koker, they slept, as in a trance. But still they returned night after night to stare in wonder as that strange, mysterious woman.

At last something happened—something the old people always said would happen—a man fell in love with the water woman. Some say he was from Salem. Some say he came from Naamryck. Others say he hailed from Parika, not far from the koker. Where he came from is not definitely known, but it is certain that he was a young man, tall and dark and big, with broad shoulders. His name was John, and they called him Big John because of his size.

When Big John had first heard of Water Mama he laughed and said she was a jumbie. But as time went by he heard so many strange things about her that he became curious. And so one moonlit night he went to the koker to look at the water woman.

He had waited for nearly an hour, and watched the moonlight shining on the koker and the river. His old doubts had returned and he was about to leave when he saw something strange, something that 'mek he head rise', as the old folks say when telling the story. He saw a naked woman, sitting near the koker. A moment before, he had seen no one there. Then suddenly he saw this strange woman sitting in the moonlight and combing her long, black hair. It shone brightly in the moonlight.

Big John made a few steps towards her to see her more clearly. Then suddenly she was gone. Without even turning her head around to look at him, she plunged into the river with a big splash and vanished. Where he had seen her sitting, there was a pool of water. And then arose a strong, fishy smell. A feeling of dread overcame him.

He then set out to get away from there. He tried to run but could only walk. And even as he began walking, his steps were slow and his eyes were heavy with sleep. And that is the way he went home, walking and staggering, barely able to open his eyes now and then to see where he was going, walking and sleeping, as in a trance.

The next morning when Big John awoke and remembered what he had seen and experienced the night before, he became afraid. He vowed never to go back to the koker to look at the water woman. But that night the moon rose, flooding the land in silver, glistening in the trees, sparkling on the river. He became enchanted. His thoughts turned to the riverside and the strange woman combing her long, black hair.

And so later that night he stood near the koker waiting and watching for the strange woman to appear. Just like the night before, she appeared suddenly near the koker, combing her hair in the moonlight. Big John stepped towards her but she plunged into the river and disappeared. And once again he had that feeling of dread, followed by drowsiness as he walked home.

This went on for several nights, with Big John becoming more and more fascinated as he watched the water woman combing her hair in the moonlight. After the third night he no longer felt afraid, and he walked in the pool of water she left behind. Sometimes he waited until morning and searched around for locks of her hair and her comb, but he never found them.

After a few months of this waiting and watching, Big John felt sad and lost. He had fallen in love with the strange woman. But he could not get near to her. And so he stopped going to the riverside to watch her.

When the moon had gone and the dark nights came back he began to drop her from his mind. But in another month the moon returned, flooding the land in silver, gleaming in the trees, sparkling on the river, and he remembered the water woman, and he longed to see her combing her hair again.

And on that very night the moon returned, he had a strange dream. He saw the water woman sitting near the koker, combing her long, black hair shining in the moonlight. She sat with her back to the river and her full face towards him. As she combed her hair she smiled with him, enchanting him with her beauty. He stepped forward to get a closer look, but she did not move. And so at last he saw her clearly, her bright eyes, her lovely face, her teeth sparkling as she smiled, and her body below her waist tapered off like a fish. She was the most beautiful creature he had ever seen.

He stretched out his hands to touch her, and she gave him her comb and said, 'Take this to remember me by.'

Then she jumped into the river and disappeared.

When he awoke the next morning he remembered the dream. He felt happy as he told his friends what he had seen in the dream. But they were afraid for him, and they warned him:

'Is haunt she hauntin' you.'

'She goin' mek you dream an' dream till you don' know wha' to do wid youself.'

'When she ready she goin' do wha' she like wid you.'

'Big John you better watch youself wid de water woman.'

'De water woman goin' haunt you to de en'.'

These warnings made Big John laugh, and he told them:

'She can' do me anyt'ing in a dream.'

But they warned him again:

'You forget 'bout de water woman, but she don' forget 'bout you.'

'Is you start it when you watch she so much at de koker.'

'Now you 'rouse she an' she want you. Da is de story now, she want you.'

Big John laughed off these warnings and told them that nothing was going to happen to him as nothing could come from a dream.

But later that day he saw something strange. It made him shiver with dread. On the floor near his bed was a comb. He could not believe his eyes. It looked very much like the comb the water woman had given to him in the dream. He wondered how a comb he had seen in a dream could get into his room.

When he told his friends about finding the comb they said:

'Is bes' for you to go 'way from here.'

'Is you start it when you watch she so much at de koker.'

That night he had another dream. In this dream he saw the water woman sitting in the moonlight. He stepped even closer to her than before, and she smiled with him.

For the first time since he had seen her, she was not combing her hair, and she had no comb in her hand. She pulled out a few strands of her hair and gave them to him and said, 'Keep these to remember me by.' And he took them in his hands and smiled with her. In another instant she was gone with a splash into the river.

The next morning Big John awoke with a smile as he remembered the dream. But as he sat up in bed he found himself with a few strands of hair in his hands. His eyes opened wide in surprise. It was only then that he realised that he was getting caught in something strange.

And so the dreams went on, night after night. They became like magnets drawing Big John to bed early every night, and holding him fast in sleep till morning. They no longer made him feel afraid on awakening.

In one dream the water woman gave him a conch

shell. On awakening the next morning he found sand on his bed and grains of sand in both hands. One night he dreamt that he and the water woman played along the river bank, splashing each other with water. The next morning he found his bed wet, and water splashed all over the room.

Big John told his friends about these dreams, and they warned him that the water woman had him under a spell. They were right, he kept on dreaming about her night after night.

Then came his last dream. The water woman stood by the riverside holding a large bundle to her bosom. She smiled and said: 'You have my comb and strands of my hair. I have given you other little gifts to remember me by. Tonight I shall give you money to make you rich. If you keep it a secret you will stay on earth and enjoy it. If you do not keep it a secret, you must come with me and be my lover for ever.'

She hurled the bundle to him, and then jumped into the river and was gone.

When Big John awoke the next morning he found the floor of the room covered with tens of thousands of five-dollar bills, piled up high in heaps. It took him a long time to gather them and count them. It was a vast fortune.

Big John was too excited to keep the news about the dream and the fortune it had brought all to himself. He went around the village and told some of his closest friends about it. When they went with him to his house and saw those great piles of money, their eyes bulged and their mouths opened wide in amazement.

Then they made a wild scramble for it. They fought among themselves all that afternoon for the money. Some of them got away with little fortunes. Some ran away with their pockets bulging with notes. Others were left with notes that got torn up in the scrambling and fighting. Big John himself was beaten by the others and got nothing. They ran away and left him.

What happened to Big John after that no one knows. Some say he dreamt again of the water woman that night and she took him away in the dream. Some say he went to the koker several nights to look for her but never found her, and so he drowned himself in the river. Others say that the water woman sent her water people after him, and that they took him to live with her in her home at the bottom of the river.

But if you go down to the koker near Parika on any night of the full moon, you will see the water woman sitting with her back to the road and her face to the river, combing her long, black, shiny hair in the moonlight. You will also see a tall, big man with broad shoulders standing close beside her.

HOW YOU BEGAN
Amabel Williams-Ellis   30p
552 54064 1

You began from a tiny blob of jelly, smaller than the full-stop on this page. This book provides a simple but comprehensive account of the beginnings of human beings and other creatures which have developed over the centuries.

EAT WHAT YOU GROW
Malcolm Saville   30p
552 54075 7

Have you ever eaten home-grown vegetables? They are delicious and you don't necessarily need a lot of room. You can grow ridge cucumbers and tomatoes that start off in an egg box on a window ledge and mustard and cress which grows well on a flannel. You'll find many useful tips in this book.

ARCHIE—YOUNG DETECTIVE
by Robert Bateman   25p
552 52006 3

Something suddenly moves in the club-house, a shadow that shouldn't be there. Archie stops to listen. He doesn't look much like a detective, but when his best friend is accused of stealing money from the club Henry Archibald McGillicuddy gets his chance to play at being policeman.